SO WRONG – SO RIGHT

Emma Wetherford has always put her children first, remaining in a loveless marriage for their sake. When she meets Milo Kent, they both recognise their true soulmate in each other. But Milo loves his wife Wendy, and will never leave her: after sustaining life-changing injuries in an accident years ago, she is completely dependent upon her husband's care. Emma and Milo pack a lifetime of love into one week, before they must return to their responsibilities. But the power of destiny will not be denied . . .

Books by Glenis Wilson
Published by Ulverscroft:

BLOOD ON THE TURF
PHOTO FINISH
WEB OF EVASION
LOVE IN LAGANAS
THE HONEY TREE
ANGEL HARVEST
VENDETTA

Nottinghamshire-born Glenis Wilson was a scribbler from childhood. She has been a member of the Nottingham Writers' Club for 30 years, and is also a member of both the Romantic Novelists' Association and the Crime Writers' Association. In addition to her stories, her published work includes several articles for *The Lady* magazine.

Visit her website at:
www.gleniswilson.co.uk

GLENIS WILSON

◆

SO WRONG – SO RIGHT

Complete and Unabridged

ULVERSCROFT
Leicester

First published in Great Britain in 2011

First Large Print Edition
published 2015

A catalogue record for this book is available
from the British Library.

ISBN 978–1–4448–2618–0

Published by
F. A. Thorpe (Publishing)
Anstey, Leicestershire

Set by Words & Graphics Ltd.
Anstey, Leicestershire
Printed and bound in Great Britain by
T. J. International Ltd., Padstow, Cornwall

This book is printed on acid-free paper

'How much of my higher and better self is as yet unmarried?'

I had often thought of Anne Brontë's words in the past: the woman whose body lay at peace now in the little graveyard overlooking the sea at Scarborough, guarded over by the seagulls as they whirled and cried high above.

Now the words no longer applied.

Prologue

1978

She asked me to set it down, black on white. 'Make it readable,' she added. 'It's a story that should be read.'

'Why me?' I protested. 'Why not one of the boys?' Boys — hardly! All my three brothers were in their thirties. Even at twenty-three I was still very much the baby.

'Because you're the writer in the family. Four books published.'

'Only fiction, Mother. I'm no journalist.'

'You're a weaver of words.'

My mother meant it as a compliment. I took it as one.

'Besides,' she smiled fondly at me, 'we flout the usual tradition. I'm closer to you than to the boys. Oh, don't misunderstand me, Thalia. I love all my boys equally. But you and I, we seem to get inside each other's head. Actually know how each other feels. And I want you to become me as you write. It must be an honest account, however difficult a job that makes it. Anything less than the truth won't do.

'You once asked me if there was such a thing as perfect love, a love that lasts for a lifetime. Yes, my darling, there is — the true love between two soulmates. We cannot know if it is pure chance or destiny that causes us to meet. All I can say is, you will know when it happens. Love is the strongest thing in the world — it cannot be lost or severed — and when soulmates meet, there is a surety within our hearts we shall be together forever.'

PART ONE

1983

1

'I think she's gone.' Adam clenched his jaw against rising emotion. He looked tenderly down at his mother's motionless figure, seemingly lost in the big double bed. The white bedspread simulated the whiteness of her skin. Emma's blue eyes were hidden now under lowered lids. The only colour was her auburn hair, and that had lost youthful brightness, faded by all the passing years. As eldest of the four siblings, it was up to him to keep control, stay in charge. He turned his head away, a muscle twitching in his cheek. He hoped neither Ian nor Simon, his twin brothers, had noticed it. His sister, Thalia, hadn't, that was for sure. Tears were already trickling down her pale cheeks as she sat beside the bed, enfolding one of her mother's hands in both her own.

She lifted her face and looked up at him, gently shaking her head and mouthing the word 'no'.

Adam took a step forward and looked closer. Thalia indicated her hands. The fingers were resting lightly below the base of her mother's thumb, over the pulse. He nodded.

The doctor was calling again at eight o'clock, it was almost that now. He wished his father were still alive. God forgive him but he wished his mother had gone first, that way it would have been easier to cope. He'd respected his father greatly, even, in a way, loved him, but Adam acknowledged that his father's first love had been the business; the four children and his wife, Emma, had come lower down the scale. Yes, his father had been a cold man. Looking down with overwhelming love at his mother, he thanked the same God that he hadn't taken after him.

Thinking of his father triggered a memory and brought unbidden words into his mind.

'Your father coming?'

He was nine years old, back in the sweaty atmosphere of the changing room at boarding school, the air filled with the smell of excitement, hot bodies and, yes, fear too.

Jackson, his best friend, had been bending over, pulling on running shoes, struggling with the white laces, looping them, re-looping them, trying to get a firm knot.

'I don't know . . . I think he could. Yes, I think he could.' He heard his own reply, knowing as he spoke he was stalling, saving face; he knew only too well it was very unlikely.

He was in the 100 yards. He'd always been

pretty swift as a runner. Gibbs, the PE teacher, had been quick to see his potential; had run him in a few trials, picked him out, put him in this race. This would be the finale for the school year — Sports Day. His chance this time to be a shining light. Not in the field of academics. Oh no, he wasn't brainy, he acknowledged that to himself, but one thing he could do was run.

'Both Mother and Father are coming,' Jackson's voice interrupted. 'Just hope I don't make a fool of myself in front of them.'

Adam didn't say anything. Chance would be a fine thing to make a fool of himself in front of his father — he really didn't think it would happen. His father wouldn't see if he were a fool or not because he would not be present. There would be a Board Meeting or some other meeting or he'd be down on the site. There'd be something. He could even have gone abroad, he often did; short notice, flight booked — gone. Whatever else came up, work came first.

But all the same the butterflies were dancing inside him. Or, more likely, the maggots were crawling. Yes, maggots, gnawing away at him, his nerves playing hell as they always did before some big occasion, keying him up, helping the adrenalin to flow possibly, but still chewing him to pieces. But it gave him the edge and he threw the whole of himself, body, mind and spirit, into whatever he was about to do.

His running shoes were securely double knotted now — all ready. He did a few running steps on the spot, punching out, so keyed up now he couldn't remain still.

But the bursting energy within him had only really been released in that last 20 yards.

Head to head, O'Roirdon and he had fought it out. Stride, stride, stride and so slowly, inch, inch, inch he had drawn away. And the tape had been coming up closer and closer and closer. Then he'd found the extra, that tiny drop of petrol left in the tank, the zoom of the rocket star, the defiant last one, a whoosh and then a burnout as he'd gone through the tape first, dropping to his knees gasping, almost retching, for breath. His heart had been singing with pride knowing he had won the last race of the year.

He was vaguely aware of the parents cheering and clapping as they watched from the side lines. And then Jackson was through, cannoning into him, fetching both of them down, rolling on the dry grass, picking themselves up, lurching forward still spent in breath but high in soul and spirit, clinging to each other, laughing, gasping, staggering down to the bottom of the track.

The parents were waiting, arms reaching, faces smiling, voices praising, roars of delight. And there was Jackson's mother and his father.

Jackson gave a wail of anguish. His father had a leg encased in plaster.

'It's OK, son, just a stupid accident. I didn't think I'd get out of the bloody hospital in time, was waiting for hours, but I managed it.'

And Adam saw the strong hand come down firmly, grip Jackson's bony shoulder where his collarbone protruded from the vest. Dragged his gaze away, looked in front. Where were they?

A sea of faces swam before him. And then a bulky, awkward figure moved forward, not fast, but towards him. Dressed in a loose, blue shift, auburn hair swinging about her shoulders, arms held wide, he saw his mother, just his mother, just his heavily pregnant mother. He could have wept, but didn't. The love shining from her eyes lifted him right at the moment when he could have broken and he went into the encircling arms, laying his head against her. Felt her soft cheek come into contact with his own.

'Well done, son!'

Adam opened his eyes. Saw his mother where she lay on the bed. Was unaware he had closed his eyes, had been back in the body of that nine-year-old all those years ago. How many years? Twenty-five? No. He looked across at Thalia, it must be twenty eight. With a shock he realised his mother had been eight months pregnant with his sister that long ago Sports Day.

Now, standing beside the bed where his mother lay so very ill, he was no longer a child but a grown man, thirty seven years old, the one all the others were relying upon.

Beside him his twin brothers moved awkwardly, uncomfortably, almost as one. They did everything together. A most unlikely looking pair of twins: Ian, tall, raw-boned with deep red — you couldn't call it auburn — hair, cut short in wiry curls, and his twin, tall also, but with his father's black hair. Both so unalike in appearance and yet inside they were one.

'Sounds like the doctor's arrived.' Ian's blue eyes sought his urgently, relief clearly written in them now Adam had mentally returned to take charge of the situation. 'I'll go and let him in?'

Adam nodded.

★ ★ ★

They were all four gathered in the kitchen.

The doctor came back downstairs, placed

his black bag carefully on the table and straightened to look at them.

'She's more than holding her own. In fact, she seems quite a lot stronger. Her pulse is better and yet, she is still in deep coma. There's nothing more I can do. She refused to go to hospital. It's simply a case of wait and see now. The District Nurse is in twice daily monitoring her drips, etcetera.

'You have my number. If there is any change, please feel free to call me at any time, day or night.'

Adam, acting as spokesman for all of them, voiced the question they hardly dared ask. 'Doctor . . . is there even a slim chance that my mother — our mother — might pull through?'

There was a heavy silence in the kitchen. The doctor spread his hands and said wearily, 'I don't know. I'm not God, I don't know all the answers. A lot of it, in this sort of case, comes down to willpower, how much your mother wants to fight — to go on living.'

'Is there anything at all, even the slightest thing,' Thalia said, 'to tip the balance?'

Simon spoke, or it could have equally been Ian, and said for them all, 'We love her very much. If there is any help we can give . . . please, tell us.'

They waited, their desperation charging the

atmosphere with taut expectancy.

The doctor reached for the handle of his black bag. 'Be with her, talk to her, maintain contact. That is the best thing you can do. If there is something of especial emotional importance you can say to give her the will to go on, it could be a major help.'

'Thank you.' Adam swallowed hard. 'I'll show you out.'

The other three remained silent until Adam returned.

'So?' Ian looked at his eldest brother. 'What do we do? It looks like it's up to us.'

Adam began pacing up and down, dragging fingers through his dark hair. 'I wish to God I *could* think of something.'

Simon slammed a fist down impotently onto the kitchen table. 'Emotionally important he said — and I've no bloody idea at all.' He looked helplessly at his twin, who shook his head.

Thalia rose to her feet. 'I know something.'

The three men stared at her.

'It's something very shocking, yet very wonderful, too. It will certainly change all our lives, forever, but it might bring Mother back to us.'

Adam ceased pacing. 'Go on.'

Thalia dashed a hand across a lock of blonde hair that had escaped from the broad wooden slide at the nape of her neck. 'It's something that only Mother and I know about. She asked me to set it down. It was to be handed over to you all in the event of her death.' She choked a little on the last word. 'But I think the time to read it to all three of you is now, in her room. Maybe she'll hear me, telling you.'

Ian put an arm around her shoulders. 'Just what is this?'

'What are you talking about, Thalia?' Simon shook his head in bewilderment.

'It's a fragment . . . ' she began, then shook her head firmly. 'No, not simply a fragment — it's the major part of Mother's life. She had a secret she kept from everyone, even from me — until the car crash five years ago when Father was killed and she was so badly injured. You know, she lay for a long time in that bedroom,' Thalia tipped her head upwards, 'and most of the time I was here in the house looking after her, seeing to all her physical needs. But there was another need which had to be attended to. Equally as much.

'Each afternoon she made me sit beside her bed and write down what she said. I tried to do it without sitting in judgment, tried not to interrupt, just wrote it word for word as she begged me to do. I know when I started the writing Mother really thought she might not

13

get well again and she didn't want to die leaving a secret. That's why she opened her heart to me. But she did recover. Then she pleaded that I keep the secret between the two of us as long as she was alive.

'If I read the journal now I shall be breaking my promise, but if it saves Mother's life . . . '

Simon interrupted. 'Where is this journal?'

'Locked inside my writing bureau.'

Thalia had not taken her eyes from the men's faces. She had watched bewilderment, unease, incredulity and a touch of anger cross all their faces. Now they were just blank, looking at her, waiting.

She walked to the door. 'Let's do what the doctor said — give Mother something to hold onto. Try to give her back the will to live.'

★ ★ ★

When they were gathered in a semi-circle around her mother's bed, Thalia laid the thick journal on top of the bedspread. Taking a deep breath she leaned forward and took her mother's hand.

'Mother, it's Thalia, can you hear me? The three boys are here, too. We love you, Mother, we want you to come back to us. We don't want you to die.

14

'I'm going to read them your journal. I've waited five years, I'm not going to wait any longer. Now is the right time.'

Was it imagination or was there the faintest of tremors in the thin hand? Even Thalia couldn't truthfully answer.

Still holding her mother's hand, she turned the cover and opened the journal.

PART TWO

1954

2

Is it wrong to pray for something you want?

It was a question I'd asked myself all the way to the church. Taking the dusty footpath through the fields, I walked past the tiny general store fronting Main Street and turned into Vicarage Lane.

The church rising up in front of me so solidly permanent and attuned to the surroundings seemed to be growing up through the earth rather than built upon it. Just looking at the building helped to steady the yearning restlessness within me.

The church was bounded by a low stone wall. Between the stones the mortar had crumbled away with age, leaving gaps and crevices into which ivy thrust tendrils. It scrambled and tangled rampantly over the soft, honey-coloured stone, cloaking the wall in variegated green. And set snugly into the wall was the lych gate. I put my hand on the iron handle, pushed open the gate and passed under the arch into the churchyard.

I walked slowly up the flagged path winding through the roughly cut grass. Here and there in the patches where it had been left totally untouched, wild flowers bloomed: the purple of thistle heads, rich gold of ragwort, purple-pink spires standing tall of rose bay willow herb, the tissue paper scarlet petals of poppies and sprinkled like snow, the ubiquitous ox-eye daisies.

The gravestones stood proud or not so proud. Some were so old that they leaned drunkenly towards each other as though sharing secrets. Most of the wording had been obscured now down the years — some covered with moss, some cracked, all telling of the departure of a human being from this earth.

The atmosphere was filled with a stoic acceptance for lives lived out their full designated span of days. It was a place of perfect calm. I felt touched by the peace and humbly walked along that winding path and stood before the church. I didn't know whether it would be open or not — I hoped it would be. I entered the little porch, lifted the catch on the heavy oak door and, blessings, it swung inwards and I stepped inside. There was no-one there.

The late afternoon sun slanted through the chancel windows picking out the blues, the reds, the gold of the stained glass, dappling the pews, the light suddenly catching the huge brass eagle with widespread wings which held the bible on Sundays, transforming it into burnished gold.

I walked over the ornate, iron grating of the aisle, my sandals making a hollow, echoing noise, emphasised by the deep silence within the empty church. I stood before the altar and wondered why I had come, what had brought me here, I, who had enough to eat, warmth in winter, clothing, a lovely home and three sons. I was an ungrateful bitch. I had come here to ask God for more.

Sitting down in the front pew I bent my head. The need was still strong within me. Closing my eyes, I prayed. 'Dear Father, if it be possible, I ask that I may be allowed to have another child, a daughter. A little girl to look after . . . to love . . . '

There, the words were out, dropped like tiny pebbles into a lake where they could continue to send out ripples, they could not be taken back. They were said. I had made my plea before God. Couldn't retract — didn't want to retract. I was slowly filled with a surety, a joyful anticipation.

I stood up and revelled in this uplifting feeling. Was this God answering my prayer? Telling me that it would come to pass that I would indeed have a daughter? I didn't know, but I walked back down the echoing aisle and out of the church with my head held high, like my spirits, feeling happier than I had felt for a very long time.

Perhaps that was when the story really began but then, who can say at which point anything begins? The past paves the way to the future. Without the past being as it was, the future could not be as it will be.

My birth was legitimate, my parents already married, but whether or not I was begotten from love, I cannot say. If I had to give an answer to this it would probably be 'yes', because in her own way, my mother did have a fondness for my father. But if she was happy with him it was a very fleeting happiness.

When I was five my father found another woman for whom he felt a stronger love. And then one day he was gone. From that day our lives changed, my mother's and mine.

We moved out of our home, which was a farm worker's cottage surrounded by fields. I was very much a country child. But after Father left we had to leave — it was a tied cottage.

My mother rented a small flat in the nearby town and I had to change schools.

Every evening after school, I was collected by another mother who was also collecting her own child and I had to wait at their house until my mother finished her day's work and came to fetch me.

My mother changed from a placid person, content with life, to someone who was bitter, always tired, always struggling and always worried about money.

We would wait on Saturday afternoons until the last few minutes before the street market stalls packed up and then she would go out, taking me with her, to buy the last remnants of fruit and vegetables that were going cheap. And I would see the ashamed, downcast look in her eyes and wonder how we had come to this point. Even in my childish mind I knew it was because my father was gone.

I remember one Saturday, vividly. We had gone down to the market as usual looking for some reasonable vegetables that might be left.

One of the stallholders, a stubbly-chinned man named Harry, spotted Mother. 'Hey Lucy, I know'd you'd be comin' round right on packing-up time.' He waved a grimy hand. 'Down there, on t'other end of stall, there's a good cabbage, saved it for you.'

I heard my mother catch her breath, saw her chin jut upwards. 'I'm obliged to you,' she muttered.

She was crying quietly when we arrived back home. Flinging the door closed behind us, she snatched the cabbage from her bag and hurled it with all her force at the wall.

I remember clutching her arm in fright and asking what was the matter with it. She didn't answer me, just shook her head violently and teardrops flew off the end of her chin. I couldn't understand it at the time but I guess it symbolised to her just how low we'd sunk.

I grew up learning to make do, to look for clothing bargains at jumble sales, and becoming quite skilled with the old, hand-operated sewing machine of my mother's that had originally been my grandmother's, using the end-of-roll pieces of material from the market that no-one else wanted.

Perhaps it gave me a good grounding in knowing the values of life. All I knew at the time was that other young teenage girls from my school would go round the shops with money to spend and I couldn't.

All that ended, of course, when I left school. I had to earn money. When I met Charles, I'd taken the only job offered, kitchen assistant at the nearby Golf Club, and had the job of serving out food to the members.

Charles arrived to play golf one day and came into the Club House for some refreshment. I suppose in my black and white uniform, I did look smart. Of course, working with food, I had to tie back my shoulder-length, auburn hair. The first time I saw Charles he leaned against the serving hatch and looked hard at me.

'I like girls with long hair,' he said and that was how it started.

Startled, I looked up as I handed over the food. I saw a tall man, probably mid-thirties, with dark hair curling slightly over his white polo shirt collar. He was lean of feature with dark eyes, and in those eyes I saw a look which I had seen before. It mirrored that in the eyes of Johnny Rochford.

Johnny was a boy who had left school at the same time as I had. Johnny and I had gone for walks together. He had progressed to asking me to go to the cinema but I hadn't had the courage yet to ask Mother if I might do so. I liked Johnny. I had a warm feeling in my stomach whenever I thought about him — and the look in his brown eyes. That same look was in this man, Charles Wetherford's eyes, too.

'You're a new girl here, aren't you? What's your name?' he asked, smiling at me.

'It's Emma. Yes, I've just started. It's my first week.'

'Straight from school?'

'Yes, that's right.'

'Do you live in the town?'

I nodded, blushing furiously. I felt gauche, awkward. I was unaccustomed to this sort of attention from a mature man. With Johnny it was exciting, frivolous almost, fun. But I knew with this man in front of me it wouldn't be like that. Even with all my inexperience I could sense a deeper current running through him and it unnerved me.

He picked up the plate of sandwiches, stared at me again and said, 'I shall doubtless see you tomorrow.'

And I was left watching his broad shoulders as he walked back to a table.

*   *   *

That evening whilst Mother and I sat listening to the radio there was a knock on the door. It was Johnny Rochford, tall, thin, with a cowlick of brown hair flopping over his forehead.

'Hi,' he said nervously, scuffling his feet. 'I, er . . . I wondered if you'd like to come out? Just a walk, maybe . . . could go to the cinema if you'd like, see a film . . . '

Before I could answer, Mother came through from the other room and stood just behind me. 'Won't you ask the young man in, Emma?' There was question in her voice and

26

I knew it meant he was going to get the third degree.

As she handed him his second cup of tea, she was already well into the questions. She'd discovered his age, his family, where he lived and now she was going for a bit more. 'What sort of job do you do then, Johnny?' she asked, taking a genteel sip of her tea.

Johnny buried his nose in his cup, scarlet with embarrassment. He was not the only one who was scarlet, I was too. I didn't know how to stop her pumping him for all this information and I squirmed on my chair and wished to goodness Johnny had never turned up. But Mother in full flow was impossible to stop.

'You have got a job, haven't you?' she probed.

'Er, yes, yes I have.'

'Oh good.' She brightened a little. 'Tell me, what is it?'

'I'm a packer, a packer down the Co-op, in the stores.'

'Oh.' You could practically see the steam that came up from her cup of tea freeze as she looked down at it. 'Not thinking of taking any exams or further education . . . or anything? Nothing else that you want to do as a trade, or possibly, a career even?'

'Er, no, no . . . I'm not clever enough for

27

that, I'm afraid,' he laughed nervously, passing it off.

'Well, if we're going out,' I said, 'we shall miss the start of the film shan't we, if we don't go soon?'

The look from my mother's eyes stayed me in my tracks. 'You surely don't want to go out? We're having such a nice evening in, such a nice cosy chat.'

Johnny and I exchanged looks of desperation.

'I think I'll just finish my tea and er . . . get back,' he blurted out. 'I've just remembered there's something I've got to do.'

'Oh really?' my mother purred. 'Well, now isn't that a shame. But of course,' she swooped upon his cup and saucer and relieved him of it, 'we mustn't detain you. I'm sure Emma will see you again — one day.'

And she showed him out.

'You were horrid to him, Mother,' I burst out. 'Asking him all those questions.'

'I've got to think about your future. No good getting yourself tied up with somebody content to be a *packer!*' She practically spat the word at me. 'What you need is somebody who knows where he's going and knows that he's going to get there.'

That man was Charles.

From the moment we met, he knew what

he wanted and knew he was going to succeed. And what he wanted was me.

There was never any doubt in my mother's mind, from the first evening Charles drew up in the street outside our flat in his Daimler. She practically had the red carpet out before he climbed from the car.

I don't know what attracted Charles to me except that I was very young and naïve and had no experience of men at all, apart from poor Johnny Rochford, who was, according to my mother, history.

She kept dinning it in to me. 'Look at our background. Look how I've had to struggle and scrape. The ends hardly meet despite all the hours in the day and all the work. Don't you want something different? Never mind all these highfalutin' thoughts of romance. What you need, my girl, is a steady, dependable man.'

And despite Charles' faults — and really he hadn't many — he could certainly be described as that. As a caring human being, he could not. Materially, yes, he provided and provided very well. Looking back, I saw even playing golf was not for recreational purposes as far as Charles was concerned. It was simply an extension of business. The golf course was a place for meeting business acquaintances, for furthering deals in convivial, relaxed surroundings, well-oiled by drinks in the nineteenth after the game.

When our boys came along I had thought that would be enough. But when the first bloom of motherhood had worn off and Charles had insisted on packing Adam off to boarding school when he was eight, and the twins were approaching five years old and would be starting at the infant school any day now, I saw my future stretching out aridly in front.

I would have been quite content to be a wife and mother had everything been reasonably all right between Charles and me. But Charles, if he had his shirts ready and his meals prepared perfectly, scarcely noticed that I was there.

After his father's fatal heart attack, the business became solely Charles' concern. For him it meant everything.

I could count on one hand the number of times we made love in the year before the twins started school. I had at one point wondered very briefly if Charles actually had a mistress. But deep down I knew he didn't. Perhaps I could have coped better if he had. What I couldn't cope with was the disinterested coolness.

The day I played the strong lady and took my twin boys aged five to school for the first day before returning home to the empty house, was when it really hit. No way could I kid myself I was a strong lady. Inside me yawned a gaping pit. It was this gnawing emptiness inside which had prompted my steps and led me down to the church that hot June afternoon.

I knew it was a selfish motive, not the right reason whatsoever to think of having another child, but the desperation of looking into a future without love was untenable.

I thought if I could have a girl the two of us could become close and it would be enough, possibly — that somehow it would make up for the lack of a loving husband. And when my daughter arrived, that tiny baby gave me something to hold on to.

What is that saying? God gives — and God takes away. Indeed, I have found this to be true.

Whether God did intervene that evening only He knows.

A few nights after I had been down to the church, Charles had been playing yet another of his interminable rounds of golf, an evening game this time, where apparently the whisky had flowed copiously afterwards in the Clubhouse. But more importantly to Charles, he had secured a deal. It had been in the balance for several weeks and finally it had gone to Charles' firm.

That night when he returned home for once he was not so inhibited. I welcomed his love with open arms. A surge of happiness swamped me when I realised his tenderness to me was still there underneath the cold shell. And we were just for once as we had been on our honeymoon, the only time that Charles had really shown me a truly loving side to himself. We had been away in Jersey and there was no possibility of the business intruding between us. And so it was on this night, and I rejoiced in his passion for me, allowed myself to release all my feelings which had been pent-up for so long.

I found myself with hot tears of joy trickling slowly from the corners of my eyes onto the pillow when, finally, Charles withdrew from me. He had rolled over exhausted and immediately gone into a deep sleep. I prayed again at that moment I might bear a child born of this love.

Twice before I'd been pregnant and my nipples had smarted about a week after conceiving. This time, four days after our love-making, my nipples felt on fire.

I didn't allow myself the indulgence of anticipating anything. Not even when I had gone past my twenty eight days. It seemed as though it would be a bad omen if I were to convince myself in these first few weeks before I had any proof. But after the fourth week passed and the fifth and sixth and still there was no sign, a deep, burning joy rose within me.

After the seventh week I began to feel nauseous in the mornings and then and only then did I go to see my local doctor. I needed to know definitely about this child — this child borne from prayers and deep love.

Charles had not touched me since. Seemingly, he had satiated himself that night and he was as deeply immersed in his business as ever he had been.

I left the surgery with the doctor's words resounding in my head.

'Well, Mrs Wetherford . . . ' He'd placed his fingertips together, made a pyramid on top of his desk, his eyes twinkling at me across the broad spread of mahogany between us. 'I think this is going to bring you a great deal of happiness . . . '

'I'm actually pregnant?' I interrupted him eagerly, my eyes seeking his for confirmation.

He smiled, his eyes softening. 'Oh yes, indeed you are. About six weeks or so.' He stood up to show me out. 'Somehow, I don't think you'll be needing those tranquillisers any more, do you?'

'No,' I said and shook his hand. 'Thank you, doctor.'

* * *

I waited that evening until Charles and I were in our bedroom and then I told him.

He stopped, one leg lifted, still peeling off his second sock. Swinging round, he stared at me, a red flush starting at the bottom of his neck, suffusing upwards. 'A baby?'

'Yes, Charles, I'm expecting your baby.'

'But,' he frowned, 'we haven't . . . '

I went and put my arms around him. 'Remember that night?'

'What night?' He frowned, shaking his head as though to clear it, looking bewildered.

I so wanted him to be pleased and yet all he could think about was when had it happened. Possibly when had he been careless? I stamped on the thought as soon as it came into my mind. Of course Charles would be pleased. He had to be pleased.

'You remember,' I squeezed him a little tighter, 'you must remember?'

He rubbed his forehead. 'No, I don't remember. I've been busy, very busy, lately. Are you sure? I mean, it couldn't be a mistake, perhaps the doctor . . . '

'Charles,' I said, 'it was the night you

played golf with the chairman of the MacKenzie Company, secured the right financial details you wanted so you could go ahead and close the deal.'

The frown lifted immediately. 'Aah,' he said, his face brightening, 'the twenty-fifth.'

'Yes,' I said joyfully. Now he would be prepared to accept the idea of a new baby in the house.

'Now I remember, it was a very good night.'

I smiled happily up at him.

He chuckled. 'Losing on the golf course is worth any amount of office meetings. It's going to bring in a lot of new business to the company, that deal.'

Two days later I began to bleed.

3

I had felt uncomfortable, a niggling pain, low down. Had gone to the bathroom. I stared in sick horror at my white panties. There was a scarlet stain spreading across the crotch. I grabbed the washbasin for support. 'No! No, I don't believe it ... I don't believe it.' I heard the rising note of hysteria in my own voice. 'This child's special, I need her ... '

I went straight to the bedroom and lay down on the bed. Maybe if I lay flat it would stop. My heart was hammering inside and I was sweating freely. I willed my body to remain inert. But I couldn't stop my brain from whirling around, the terrors crowding in on me. 'Please God ... let me have this child. I need her so much.' I knew this mental churning was, if anything, worse than physical activity, but whilst I could will my body to remain perfectly still, I could not control my thoughts. They whirled in a helpless kaleidoscope of jumbled fear and desperation.

And all the time I could feel a warm, sticky seepage from my body.

Although I didn't voluntarily move, my body was trembling all over, the sweat icily cold against my skin. Pain, gasp-inducing in intensity, was taking great, gnawing bites at the soft, vulnerable flesh of my belly. Wave after wave of nausea swept over me and I daren't lift my head in case I actually started retching because that would surely release the so slight hold my baby still had on life. For nearly an hour I lay there suffering physical and mental agonies before I could accept I *was* actually having a miscarriage and needed expert help — quickly. I knew I had to get up but dare not swing my legs from the bed, fearing what might happen if I did.

The life of my tiny baby was simply draining away from me and the longer I lay there hopelessly willing it to stop, the less chance it had of seeing life. I must ring for help.

Reaching out to the side table, I groped for the phone and caught the bedside lamp with my hand sending it crashing to the floor. My fragile nerves seemed to shatter in sympathy with the light bulb and I caught back a scream. Shaking with fright, I snatched at the receiver and dialled emergencies.

★　★　★

37

I lay numb, frozen between the stiff, white sheets. All about me was the hum of activity that is always present on a hospital ward. Although part of me felt dead, perversely, another part within my head was making sense of the noises. I could close out the world, as I was doing, by keeping my eyes closed, but I couldn't close my ears. There were light treads, quick ones, some slightly heavier, one with a distinctive squeak as a particular nurse walked past. The swish of curtains, cloaking off a bed and its occupant from the outside world. The rattle of trolley wheels foretelling food, drinks . . . another woman being wheeled back unconscious from the theatre by a porter? Part of me registered quite clearly all these sounds. I had been in a maternity and a gynae ward before — I had borne three children.

But I would not bear this fourth one — and part of me was dead, too.

But the cliché, life goes on, must surely have started life in either a maternity ward or an old people's home, coming fresh into this earthly world or setting forth bravely into the next. Certainly, the immediate world around me didn't share my negativity.

Sheets were pulled straight, corners exactly mitred, stray drinking glasses clinked and cleared away. The atmosphere changed, became charged with an intangible buzzing below the surface, an expectancy in the air. 'Doctor's on his way.' Gentle admonishments. 'We want the ward looking nice, don't we? Come along, Mrs Huggett . . . ' The activity progressed down the ward.

At the side of me, presumably within the enclosed cloistered little world behind the curtains, was a rhythmic sobbing, punctuated by little, sniffling chokes as it was tried to be contained. The shoes with the squeak came bustling up. A curtain swished as the nurse entered into that private world of misery. There was the murmur of muted words, gentle words, and slowly the sobs ceased. I could almost hear myself thinking at least here, someone cares. And I felt a warmth spread up inside me for Squeaky Shoes, whoever she was.

I couldn't cry. The tears seemed too far below the surface. So I lay stiff with misery unable to experience the relief their release would bring.

And then footsteps were approaching — one unmistakable, heavy regular, the others lighter. The part of my brain that was still working noted that it was the doctor with attendant nurses. And that part of me monitored his slow progress down the ward as he checked each of his patients, bed by bed. His footsteps approached my own bed and there was a swirl of air as the nurse twitched the curtain round.

'Good morning, Mrs Wetherford. I'm Mr Milo Kent, your consultant. How are you feeling?'

There was genuineness in the query but all my frustrated bitterness surged up and I felt my eyes fly open and then I was saying awful things.

'How the hell do you think I feel? I've just lost my baby. What do you expect me to feel like? Oh, it's all right. I'm on top of the world, absolutely bloody marvellous.' To my shame, as I saw the compassion in his eyes, I burst into wild tears.

He pulled up a chair at the side of the bed, dipped a hand into the box of tissues on top of the locker and fished one out. He held it towards me. 'Have this.'

He waited as I clutched the tissue to my face as the storm of grief spent itself. I dabbed up the runs of tears from my cheeks and cautiously looked up at him. The anger was still there and the pain but now, added to it, I felt embarrassment.

'I'm sorry . . . I didn't mean . . . '

His face softened. 'It's quite all right. I *do* understand.'

And I looked into his eyes and felt a

strange kinship. It isn't able to be described, this feeling, this linking current, but kinship best expresses what I felt. And even though the pain of loss was still carving my insides to pieces, I reached out to his soul with my own and we touched on a higher level, gained comfort from it.

It is a well-accepted concept that men fall for their nurses and women for their doctors, but this wasn't the same — not at all.

He stood up abruptly, stepped back. 'You've lost a lot of blood, Mrs Wetherford. You have had a blood transfusion and you're understandably still very weak. Try to rest.' Then he left, moving on to the next patient.

I slid down under the sheet oddly comforted — not the little self, oh no, that still berated and lashed out, flailed and was, of course, totally ineffectual — but I was able to step aside from that and go into a deeper more peaceful part of myself and shortly I dozed off.

The rest of that day I spent in a twilight world half asleep and half awake, rousing every time there was a loud disturbance — and there were plenty of them.

When the trolley came round rivalling Nurse Squeaky Shoes, the part of me that was detached, practical, still working despite everything, said, why don't they get the oil

41

can round that wheel? I felt a hysterical bubble of laughter catching at the back of my throat and knew that my grip on myself was very fragile.

One of the highlights in hospital is the evening meal and the other patients were all sitting up expectantly, those that could, when the trolley came round again. The drifting smell of the cooked food permeated down the corridor and into the ward. But just the smell of it made me feel nauseous.

'You have to eat, y'know.' The kindly ward assistant in her trim green overall, straining somewhat around her ample bosom as she bent over me, plopped the covered plate down on the movable table across the bed.

'Thank you,' I said and shut my eyes. She clattered knife and fork.

'You get it down you, love, you need all your strength.' And she pushed the trolley on to the wan looking girl in the next bed.

All through the next noisy twenty minutes or so as cutlery rattled against thick hospital crockery, I lay there with my eyes closed. The comfort that I had gleaned momentarily from the consultant earlier in the day had long since dissipated and I had sunk once more into a deep pit.

When the meal ended there was the customary quietening down period just prior to the perambulation to the toilets and bathrooms for those who could and calls for the bedpan where they couldn't, all building up to that long awaited moment when the hand of the clock at the far end of the ward touched seven and the bell rang for visiting.

I turned on my side facing away from the door through which the visitors were now streaming. I didn't want to see anyone. Particularly not Charles. There was the usual buzz of subdued greetings, footsteps hesitant, quickening as the visitors located loved ones they were seeking. 'All those different floors . . . what a maze of corridors . . . didn't think I'd find you . . . oh, there you are,' — very heartfelt — 'wouldn't have recognised you, all these ladies . . . ' The comments spilled out, overlapped, turning into a generalised hubbub of conversation. A few minutes behind the main tide of visitors there were one or two stragglers. And just when I thought, selfishly, I had escaped making all that effort to communicate, maybe to even reassure someone else when it was I that needed reassurance, my mother arrived.

Unceremoniously, she dumped a brown paper bag of grapes onto the locker. At one corner, the paper bag began to take on a darker look, which slowly started to spread.

There's a bad one in there, said my practical part.

'Hello, me duck.' She bent over and gave me a quick kiss on the cheek. 'How d'y'feel? Bet you're a bit down, aren't you?' She dragged up a chair with a scrape and plumped onto it. 'Dear oh dear, it's been that hot today . . . ' She fanned herself with her hand. 'My ankles are already beginning to swell up.'

A wave of desolation swept across me and I closed my eyes. 'I just don't want to talk,' I heard my unkind, selfish voice say.

''Course you don't, love, you've been through a lot, you're tired out — exhausted, really. Mind, that's a nice nightie you've got on. That's not one of your hospital issue, is it?'

I kept my eyes closed. The nightie, my sponge bag and a few bits of clothing were items I'd grabbed when the ambulance came for me. At that moment I'd been an expectant mother, now I wasn't.

'Thought I'd just pop in for a few minutes, see how you are. Well, I know it's twelve miles but there was a bus just right. Charles can't, you see. He rang me.'

At the mention of his name I'd started to take notice again instead of letting the flow of Mother's words pass over.

44

'Rang?'

'Yes, down at the sweet shop, y'know, where I work part-time. Fortunate I was there today, wasn't it?'

I felt like saying, oh yes, Mother, bloody fortunate I had a miscarriage on the day you're available to answer a phone at the sweet shop. But I didn't. 'Charles isn't coming, then?'

'No, me duck.' She shuffled a little uncomfortably on the chair. 'He says he's going to stay home y'see, and . . . soothe the boys down a bit. They're upset 'cos you're not at home, only natural, really.'

'Yes, I was always there, wasn't I?' Inside I thought, yes, always there, always available — but now I wasn't.

'Mrs Lundy brought the twins back from school and kept them at her house. Charles went over to collect them in the car, when he got back from business.' She said it, oh, so proudly. 'But he hasn't time to come, y'know, what with teas and baths and getting off to bed, so I thought I'd just pop in.'

'Yes, thanks, Mother,' I said faintly, 'I'm very grateful.' I opened my eyes just as she popped a grape into her mouth.

'Ooooh, these are lovely. Beautifully sweet. You should try some. They're just right on a hot day, like this. You don't mind, do you? Me

45

taking one or two?'

I moved my head acquiescently. She seemed to know it was an acknowledgement to go ahead — and she did. Popping them in, one after another, talking through them, and I lay there and let it all flow over me.

'Well,' she said after about half an hour, 'I'm going to go now, let you get some rest. Charles will be here tomorrow night. He says he's going to make arrangements for the boys.'

'Tell him not to bother,' I said firmly.

'I shall do no such thing. No, it's his duty. I mean, he's your husband.' She said it with the smugness of a cat eyeing a tin of Carnation.

'Yes — I know he is.'

She seemed to sense my lack of enthusiasm. 'Well . . . anyway . . . ' Picking up her shopping bag, she pushed the chair back with another loud scrape that had heads turning. 'Righto, me duck, I'm going because I think I should about manage to pick up a bus.'

Irrationally, I felt hysteria sweep over me as my tortured imagination visualised Mother carrying a red Trent bus under her arm.

'Not very frequent, are they, buses? I might not get over again, y'know.'

'Please, Mother, there's no need, really . . . none at all. I shall be home soon.'

'Yes, that's right, you will. Back home in

the bosom of your family, again. Best place.' She leaned over, gave me another quick kiss and was gone.

Weakly, I slid down again under the welcome comfort and protection of the sheet and began to doze off. But not before I saw the stain on the brown paper bag had spread all the way round now and a glutinous liquid was trickling along the formica top of the bedside locker.

★ ★ ★

The day shift came on duty early relieving the lovely nurse who had come round in the night and helped me with a glass of water.

'We won't put the light on,' she whispered, 'some of the others have managed to go to sleep.'

'You're all very kind,' I said, meaning the nurses, 'I don't know how you keep your spirits up in here.'

'Like your knickers, love, you've got to, haven't you?' And she was gone again.

I'd been awake for so long in the night the only thing I felt like doing was dropping off to sleep. But you've got to be pretty strong to survive hospital life.

The long ago yet still-remembered routine began. Temperatures taken, arms pumped for blood pressure checks, end of bed charts rattled, filled in, pulses felt. Bright, jolly voices when all most of us wanted to do was die. It was an exhausting schedule for both nurses and patients. And later in the morning came that hint of electricity in the air, the almost palpable anticipation — the doctor was on his way. And this time I didn't close my eyes.

The doors at the far end under the clock swung open and I lay there and waited for his approach. I don't know what I expected him to say to me, but his words certainly weren't what I anticipated. At the sight of him, stupidly, I felt warm tears ooze up in the corners of my eyes, hated myself for the weakness but couldn't stop them.

When it came to my turn, he studied my chart before looking down at me. 'Not still crying, surely?' This time his voice wasn't quite so compassionate. Childishly, I felt a quick flare of self-pitying anger but it burnt out almost instantaneously.

'I think you should try getting up a little today. You'll feel stronger in the long run. I suggest you try to make your way down the ward. Why not have a chat with Mrs Huggett? She could do with a friendly word.'

'Is that doctor's orders?' I managed to say, falsely trying to be bright.

Seeing through the attempted bravado, he smiled and the warmth was back in his eyes again. 'Oh, I think you could say so.' He walked away to the next patient.

⋆ ⋆ ⋆

Lunch arrived. Very basic. Two thin, horribly contorted and burned sausages, one scoop of lumpy mash and a small heap of watery cabbage, coarsely chopped and even more coarsely cooked, from which pale green water trickled around the inside rim of the plate, doing its best to act as a moat. I attempted the vegetables and ignored the cremated protein.

I suppose I should have pointed out I was a vegetarian, a lapsed one because I did eat fish, and guiltily enjoyed it, but there hadn't seemed much point since I felt so sick both at heart and stomach.

By the time I tackled the pudding, the small amount I'd actually eaten had reawakened my stomach to life, even if the rest of me still felt pretty dead, but the sponge was so hard I feared for the spoon handle and gave it up as a bad job.

After lunch the whole tone of the ward quietened. It was always a subdued atmosphere after a meal. But a short while before

49

three o'clock, there was a perking up, visibly noticeable as thoughts unanimously turned to the best bit of the day — the afternoon cup of tea. And not only to the tea but to the little bit of chat dispensed by Janet to each one of us as she poured out our cups. A bright spot in a long, grey afternoon.

I thought about Mr Kent's suggestion and made up my mind when I'd had my tea, I'd try and get down to the far end of the ward where Mrs Huggett's bed was. I suspected there was more, much more, behind the consultant's words than had appeared, created no doubt by the very lightness of voice he had used.

The clock at the far end ticked round to three o'clock and with the expectancy of children for a forthcoming treat, heads swivelled to watch for the trolley coming — and Janet.

And there she was. It was like a ray of sunshine beaming through grey clouds to everyone. Whether or not she was aware of the good she was doing us all was a mystery but certainly it was not only the skills of the doctors which helped heal our minds and bodies. Even in the menial job of serving out refreshments she had undoubtedly found a niche for her own brand of healing. She was a very necessary part of the whole.

As Janet poured my tea and bent forward to place it on the table, she winked at me. 'You know, there're only two ways to go — up or down. Take my advice, get yourself out of here, get back home to your bloke and get on with it. Another baby will take away all that deep pain.' I gaped at her. 'True, true,' she said, 'it's what you need — and I should know. I've been there myself.'

'Have you?'

'Oh yes, three times — I lost them all.' Then she winked again. 'But I'm having a lot of fun trying to get a fourth — hopefully, this time, I'll keep it.'

'You're a lot braver than I am.'

'Rubbish,' she smiled. 'First of all you have to pick yourself up, then when you go home, you'll have to lie down.' She chuckled. 'Know what I mean?' And on she went to the next patient.

There was certainly a bawdy side to the nature in a hospital ward, especially a gynae ward.

But the black humour, disguising the shining pearl of truth, had worked wonders. I felt a lot better. Just what Janet said to Mrs Huggett, I don't know, she only allowed her voice to carry to the patient she was speaking to. It was a small sign of respect for personal privacy but it was a big one for each of us.

Whatever she had said lightened Mrs Huggett's face, brought a half smile briefly to her lips. But as I sat and sipped the none-too-hot tea, I saw the light slowly dying from her face and the pinched look reappear and it didn't surprise me to see Mrs Huggett push away her half-drunk tea, turn on her side and bury her face in the pillow.

Setting down my empty cup and saucer on the bedside locker, I pushed the covers purposefully from me and swung my feet out of bed. With legs that felt like half-set jelly and with a peculiar lightness in my head, I took my first steps down the ward.

What I was going to say to Mrs Huggett I had no idea. I doubted whether I could help her in any way.

But in such a ward as this there was undoubtedly a bond of sisterhood, and I just hoped I'd find the words she needed to hear. Although I hadn't believed Mr Kent, I acknowledged when I reached the end of the ward that, strangely enough, I did feel stronger than when I'd first stepped out of bed. However, I sank down gratefully on the chair beside Mrs Huggett's bed.

'Hello,' I said to the back of her head. Initially, there was no response but when I repeated the greeting she lifted a strained, white face and looked up at me with eyes filled with haunted misery. Her naked pain pierced me almost as much as my own. 'I'm Emma,' I said softly.

She made a visible effort. 'Jane . . . my name's Jane.'

I nodded. 'We're both in the same boat, aren't we?' Involuntarily, my fingers began pleating the edge of the sheet.

'You've lost a baby, too?'

I didn't trust myself to speak so I just nodded. We seemed to sit there for a long time, bonded not only by our hands resting on the impersonal hospital bed but by an inner, intangible wavelength.

Finally, Jane whispered, 'Mine was a little girl.'

And the knife inside me turned again.

Jane's eyes held mine. 'What was yours?'

I shook my head helplessly. 'I wasn't far enough gone . . . they don't know.'

She bit her lip. 'I so wanted a baby daughter.'

At that moment I felt I could have lashed out and hit Mr Kent right in the face. If he had walked into the ward at that instant, I believe I would have done. It was all very well trying to ease another's emotional agony, but when it intensified one's own, it was asking too much. But Jane's next words erased all the resentment and ill-feeling within me, like

53

a duster drawn across a school blackboard.

'I'll never have the chance again. I can't have any more babies.' Tears welled and flowed, trickling down her cheeks, dripping onto the pillow. The disgust I felt at myself was beyond expression.

'Surely,' I began, frantically searching for some self-control, 'your other children . . . at home . . . ' I left the sentence hanging in the air. But I was appalled to see the dark head roll first to one side and then the other.

Jane said simply, 'I have no other children.'

And then I knew exactly the reasoning behind the consultant's words, 'Why not speak to Mrs Huggett? She could do with a friendly word.' It was like a healing balm to my own pain. A cauterising of the emotional wound as I had been cauterised physically. It was right then my own personal healing began.

I squeezed Jane's hand. 'I know it's not the time, the place, but . . . adoption?'

I put the query into my voice and hoped that the word would drop into her mind and lodge there and in the hours and days to follow, her subconscious would work upon it.

4

At seven o'clock the bell rang. Visitors streamed through the door. I had lain there for the previous hour hoping against hope that Charles would not be amongst them, but these hopes were in vain because there he was. At six feet two inches, he towered over most of the other visitors. In his hand he carried a bunch of flowers. Hesitating for a moment, he scanned the double row of beds. Then, spotting mine, he marched purposefully down the centre of the ward, leaned over, gave me a perfunctory peck on the cheek and pushed the bunch of flowers into my hand.

'I've brought you these to cheer you up a bit.'

I hadn't expected them and for a second it threw me. It was not in keeping with Charles' usual manner.

'Thank you, they're lovely.' And they were — gold roses. The wrapping around them had the name of the flower shop upon it — Mardel's, the most expensive flower shop in Nottingham. 'You shouldn't have, Charles. They must have cost you a fortune.'

'I've no idea,' he said casually. 'I simply gave Joanne a £20 note and told her to get something nice for you.'

The warmth that had been slowly creeping into my cold body at the sight of the flowers evaporated. Joanne was Charles' secretary. How stupid of me to think he'd actually gone to the shop himself and chosen some that he knew I would like.

Joanne knew I liked gold roses. On a previous wedding anniversary she had been instructed by Charles to buy a bouquet of my favourite flowers. She had actually asked me what my favourite blooms were.

'She's the perfect secretary,' I said and my voice sounded like a strangled whisper. 'Clever girl. She's either got a first class memory or she must keep a personal file of my likes and dislikes.' The irony in my voice was lost upon Charles.

'Yes, she has actually.' It took my breath away. I could barely believe it, especially when he continued, 'I just instruct her to give me a nudge a day or two before all the birthdays and anniversaries in the family so I don't forget.'

'So then you can tell her to buy the necessary presents?'

'That's it.'

'Of course, that's what secretaries are for,

aren't they?' I heard myself say and at the same time, felt the coldness within me deepen.

'Your mother came last night, I understand.'

'Yes.'

'Hmmm, do you know if she's coming tomorrow?'

'I don't think so.'

'Well, you see, I've asked Mrs Lundy if she would mind having the twins for a couple of hours extra tomorrow evening. There's an important golf match scheduled, business-wise, of course, and er . . . I shall be pretty well tied up. It means I can't come to visit you.'

'Quite. I understand.'

'Knew you would.' He said it complacently.

'I may be out tomorrow.'

'Really! Well, that is good news. When will you know for sure?'

'I have to wait until the doctor's rounds.'

'If he says yes, do you think you can just give Joanne a ring for me and put her in the picture? Then we can alter the arrangements for the twins.'

'Yes, of course,' I said, 'after I've rung for a taxi to bring me home.'

'Oh, oh yes, hmmm.'

We were both silent. There was really very little to say.

The intermittent burning soreness in my lower tummy, just above my pelvic bone came on again and I shifted uncomfortably in the bed, trying to ease it. Apparently, they had had to do a D. and C. after the miscarriage.

'Are you in pain?' Charles looked at me rather anxiously.

'Only a little, physically.' Our eyes met. 'Are you very upset, Charles, about the baby?' It was just possible he was hiding some deeper, painful feelings. He bent his head and inspected his perfectly clean, squarely manicured nails.

'Could they tell? Whether it was a boy . . . or a girl?'

It was the first flicker of any real interest that he had shown at all. And all the emotional pain inside me, at that point, hurt far more than the physical soreness. I shook my head. 'No.'

'I think it much better not to know.' Charles' voice was brisk now, to the point. 'Less grief for you. You'll be able to get over it quicker, well, that's how I look at it, anyway.'

I thought about Janet's words this afternoon, about trying for another baby when I went back home. Although I felt resistance rise forcibly in my throat against asking Charles, some demon inside drove me on. 'Shall we . . . try for another baby, Charles?

When I'm a bit stronger, when I'm home?' Under the bed sheets my left hand involuntarily clenched itself and I could feel the nails digging into my palm. I waited for his answer.

'We've got the three boys. I think that's enough for us, don't you?' He smiled briefly. 'Less hurtful for you that way.'

'But I would have liked a girl.' Liked a girl? It was the one thing in the world I craved for.

Charles shifted his gaze away from me to the bottom of the ward and looked at the clock. 'Girls, we-ell, I should think they could be quite a headache, much more so than boys. Especially when they get in their teens. No, I think we should be content with the three boys.' He patted my hand quickly and took a step away from the bed as if needing to put space between us in case I should throw my arms around him, cry all over him, or otherwise demonstrate any emotion.

But I didn't. I merely closed my eyes to blot out the sight of him.

'I'm very tired, Charles. I think I'll have a sleep now.'

'Oh, absolutely,' he said with relief, 'much the best thing. Get yourself well again and hurry home. That's where you should be.' He didn't go on to add washing and ironing my shirts and cooking my meals, but that's what he meant.

I didn't bother opening my eyes as he walked away.

★ ★ ★

The night was endless and I slept very little; pain in my body was a constant on/off nag, for which I suppose I could have asked for a pain killer, but I didn't bother.

It has been said that if you have a physical pain and deliberately cause another one, the two very often cancel each other out. But this doesn't seem to work when the second pain is emotional. The agony of loss was a far greater hurt than anything I had ever felt before and there were no pills that could relieve this pain.

Possibly Janet's way of thinking was right. The only way to really ease it would be to start another baby. But even had Charles been willing, I recoiled from the very thought. If I were allowed home tomorrow, I would return and take up life exactly where I'd left off. But all Charles would be to me now would be the provider. I no longer considered Charles my husband.

★ ★ ★

I opted to come home from the hospital by taxi the next day. I could have come back by ambulance but they weren't there for sole transportation. I knew there would be at least one if not two other women — and their new born babies — in that ambulance taking us all home, dropping us off one by one, literally in my case, or two by two in theirs. I couldn't face it.

It seemed an eternity of a drive sitting in the back of the droning taxi as it left the city and headed out through the Nottinghamshire countryside and down the lanes until we reached Alney. We drove in through the gates between the lions and the taxi driver drew up outside the front door.

'Thanks, thanks very much indeed.' I fumbled for the fare. 'Could I ask you, please, if you could just carry my bag inside?'

'Sure thing, ma'am,' said the huge black man, grinning widely, teeth startlingly white against the blackness of his skin. He lifted my suitcase over the doorstep and deposited it at the foot of the staircase. He flourished a small white square from an inside pocket. 'There's my card, anytime.'

'Thanks.' I added another coin to the fare and pushed it into his hand.

Closing the door behind him, I stood looking round the hall. It seemed an age since

I had been here instead of simply three days since I'd been rushed out. Kneeling down on the parquet floor, I slipped the catches on the suitcase and opened the lid. Gathering up an armful, I slowly climbed the stairs. I felt about as strong as a baby kitten. It was easier to make two, maybe three, journeys rather than lift the case upstairs in one go.

I walked into our bedroom and stood with the clothes clutched tightly to me and looked at the quilt-covered double bed with the frilled edged pillowcases. This was where the baby had been conceived and I fought down an overwhelming urge to scream and go on screaming. On wooden legs, I crossed stiffly to the chest of drawers and put my clothes away.

On the third trip I brought the suitcase up with me and put it away on top of the wardrobe. Then I sat down on my side of the bed. The night I had conceived would undoubtedly be the last time I allowed Charles to make love to me — for it *had* been love that night, a regression back to that so short blissful interlude of our honeymoon.

Now the very thought of his joining our bodies together made my stomach heave.

I jumped up and immediately regretted it. My head swam and felt as though it was taking off, leaving my body grounded behind.

I swayed and clutched the headboard and stood for a moment, fingers pressed against my temples until the giddiness subsided. And then I walked slowly down the landing to the airing cupboard, took out a pair of clean, sweet-smelling single sheets with matching pillowcase and opened the door to the guestroom. The single bed welcomed me in.

For the first time since stepping over the threshold, I felt a peace envelop me. I would simply tell Charles, I thought, as I smoothed the sheet over the mattress, that I needed total rest, total quiet which meant sleep and plenty of it. I would also tell the twins the same thing. They, of course, would accept it unquestioningly. Charles might, or then again, he might not, but it really didn't matter because that was the way it was going to be from now on.

The decision I had come to hadn't been made lightly or hastily, it was a compounded one brought about over many years. The last few days had been the proverbial straw.

Some straw.

★　★　★

Thalia stopped reading. There was no sound in the bedroom. Emma lay motionless beneath the covers in the double bed. Thalia lifted her eyes from her mother's journal and gazed at her brothers. They resembled the three graces: individual, totally united — yet frozen into immobility. She was moved with compassion for them.

It had shaken her to the very core when she had written down her mother's words in the journal five years ago. Now her brothers were going through the same shattering experiences. Knowing the revelations to come, Thalia grieved for them.

Gently, she said, 'And that's just the start.'

'Then I need a drink.' Adam scraped back his chair. His two brothers stood up in unison.

'I'll stay with Mother,' Thalia said. 'After all, I know what's coming, I wrote it down.'

PART THREE

1978

5

The phone call had come through to Pegasus Racing Stables at Waltham-on-the-Wolds at seven a.m. on the fifteenth of June, the day after Thalia's twenty-third birthday. In her box of a room in the stable lads' quarters, her half dozen cards were jostling for space on the narrow window frame and the tiny cabinet beside her single bed.

She had telephoned her mother the day before and apologised for not being able to make the fourteenth. 'Can't be helped, Mother. I'm away racing . . . Edinburgh this time, no chance of getting back. Thanks for the card, love the picture . . . I adore bluebell woods. Promise I *will* see you at the weekend. Well, weekend, you know what racing's like, Sunday certainly. Love you, love to Dad, bye.'

Arriving back from Edinburgh racecourse at a quarter to twelve that night, she had felt the usual disgruntlement common to all stable lads who arrived back this side of the big twelve following a race day. After midnight, she would have been excused early morning stables. As it was, she was still faced with a five-thirty start the next morning. She had been put down for first lot riding Juggernaut. A small blessing but one much appreciated. He was an easy ride compared to some of the racehorses.

In company with the other eight stable lads, she rode out in the pearl bright early morning, yawning widely, breathing in the clear fresh air of the new day, trying to draw some energy into her lungs. Juggernaut had been worked the previous day and apart from some jig-jogs at the start, he quickly settled and fell into line four down in the string, allowing Thalia to ease her body into the rigours of another demanding day.

Nearly an hour later, the horses' hooves clopped hollowly over the yard as the string wound back in again. Thalia threw her right leg over and slid from the horse, flicking the reins over his head. She chirruped him on and led the horse back to his stable where she began to untack. The trainer walked across and put his head over the half-door.

'Phone call for you.' The annoyance in Dickson's tone wasn't concealed.

'Right, Gov'nor.' Thalia slid the bridle over Juggernaut's ears and the spittle-wet bit from between his teeth, slipping on his head collar. Leaving him tied up, she crossed the yard to the stable office. The phone handset lay on the desk. Thalia picked it up. 'Hello.'

'That you, Thalia?' It was Adam, her eldest brother. His voice, taut and urgent, came down the line. There was a clutch at her stomach. Before he said anything further she knew it must be bad news.

'What's wrong? Something happened?'

'Come home, now, straight away, Mother needs you. There's been an accident . . . '

'Bad?'

'Very.'

'I'm on my way.'

*   *   *

The white Polo lapped up the miles from Leicestershire to Alney. Thalia drove through the main street, turned off down Buttery Lane and arrived at the entrance of the drive where her parents lived. Someone — Adam? — had left the gates open ready for her. She roared past the identical stone lions seated impassively atop the two brick pillars and depressed clutch and brake in a screeching halt outside the front door. Disturbed by the sudden rush of air, several pink petals from the climbing rose that scrambled over the porch fluttered down onto the bonnet of the car.

Back in her room at Pegasus Racing stables, a slight breeze through the partially opened window rustled Thalia's birthday cards. One rocked, hesitated, tipped over and finally fell to the floor. The bluebells on the cover made a brave splash of colour on the bare boards.

★　★　★

Adam poured a generous helping of brandy from the decanter on the sideboard in the lounge and handed it to Thalia. Her hand was shaking as she closed fingers around the glass. She took a quick gulp and the brandy sent coursing fire down her throat. 'Father?' she whispered uncomprehendingly. 'Father's . . . dead?'

'Yes.'

For a few moments she sat speechless, numb with the sense of loss. They had never been close but he had always been there in the background, a comfortable presence. She gathered herself, drained the glass, choking a little. 'What . . . what about Mother? Is she . . . ?'

'No, no, Mother is still alive. She was taken straight from the car crash to Nottingham Hospital. She's badly injured, but, thank God, she's still alive.'

'The twins, Ian, Simon . . . do they know?'

'Yes. They're over in Brussels on business.

I've phoned the hotel and they're catching the first flight home.'

Thalia struggled to her feet, legs like jelly, set down the empty brandy glass and said, 'I must go to her, immediately.'

'I know.' Adam slid a steadying hand under her elbow. 'We'll take my car. You're certainly in no fit state to drive.'

Neither of them spoke during the twenty minute drive from Alney to the hospital. As they entered the intensive care unit a clean, aseptic smell met them. The near silence was broken only by the regular tick of an IVAC and the bleeping of monitors.

The Sister came out and took them to one side. 'Mrs Wetherford is sleepy. She's heavily sedated, of course — her injuries are extensive. She's lost a lot of blood and is on a drip. The next twenty-four hours are critical.' She allowed a brief, sympathetic smile to flit across her face. 'I'm sorry, that is all I can say. Everything is being done.'

Thalia, her own face bloodless with shock and grief, whispered, 'Thank you, I'm sure it is. Could I . . . please . . . I'd like to sit with her.'

'Of course.' The nurse turned with a swish of uniform, her rubber soled shoes whispering away across the highly buffed floor.

Thalia slid into the empty seat beside the

bed. Her horrified gaze took in what little there was to be seen of her mother's face, so heavily bandaged was she. The little that remained visible was badly bruised. Thalia closed her eyes momentarily, feeling quite sick. Looking up at her brother, she said, 'Are we going to lose her, Adam? We've lost Father.'

Adam hunkered down by her side and put a strong arm around her shoulders. 'I don't know, Sis, I really don't know. She's in God's hands.'

'Tell me what happened. Do you know?'

'Not really,' he sighed heavily. 'Obviously, the car crashed.'

'What made it crash?'

'We're not sure. There's no evidence of another vehicle being involved.'

'It happened on my birthday,' Thalia shuddered. 'For evermore it's going to remind me.'

'No. Don't let it.' Adam's voice was hard. 'The crash happened, yes, but Father died in the early hours of this morning, not yesterday.'

'If Mother . . . ' Thalia gulped. 'When Mother regains consciousness, comes home, she'll need a lot of looking after.' She stroked the back of her mother's hand with gentle fingertips.

'Yes, she will.'

'I'll give up my job,' Thalia said resolutely. 'I shall come home, back to Alney and look after her, nurse her, for as long as it takes.'

Adam gripped her arm very hard, his appreciation of her sacrifice showing clearly in the love in his eyes. 'And the twins and I will take over the running of Father's business.' He released his grip and looked down helplessly at his mother. 'There's nothing we can do right now. I think the best thing to do would be to go home and wait it out there. We're going to need all our energy and stamina with the look of it. The hospital has our telephone number. They've promised to ring straight away if there is any change — either way.'

Mutely, Thalia rose to her feet and with one anguished backward glance at her mother's still form, followed Adam from the intensive care unit. Still stunned with shock, she allowed him to drive her home.

The taxi from the airport brought Ian and Simon back home to Alney at six o'clock that evening. The four of them came together in the spacious hall and reached out to each other. The four bodies became one as arms enveloped, held tightly, comforted silently.

Ian was the first to speak. 'Father — God bless him . . . ' he said brokenly. 'Mother?

73

What are Mother's chances?'

'We don't know,' Adam, replied. 'We simply pray.'

★　★　★

'I do understand.' The modulated voice of Dickson, the racehorse trainer, Thalia's employer, came down the line. 'Family is family, and you must do what you feel you have to. But, Thalia, have you considered your immediate future? I'm not saying don't stay and do your duty at that end. I am saying consider what you are giving up. How old are you now? Twenty-three? There's only another couple of years . . . '

Thalia understood perfectly well what he was getting at. In two years she would be twenty-five and at that point would lose her opportunity to obtain a jockey's licence. It had been her dream since late childhood to become a professional jockey.

'I understand what you're saying, Mr Dickson, but let's face it, I haven't got my licence yet and it's a toss-up really whether I will, isn't it? I think if I'd been going to get it, I would have by now. Yes, I know racing has been in a difficult state but perhaps I just don't have that additional edge I need.'

'You're a damn good rider.'

Thalia bit her lip. 'Thanks, but I'll finish that one for you — just not good enough.' His silence at the other end said it all.

Thalia found putting into words what she had long suspected was not an easy thing to do. Her hand was gripping the phone tellingly tightly, betraying all her inner tension. But maybe this was the ideal time to face up to the fact that whilst she might have her heart set in the racing world among her beloved horses, and the whole day to day life of racing, she was not cut out to be a star jockey.

Whether she would be content within herself to accept life on a lower rung of the ladder, riding work at the stables, leading up at the tracks, preparing horses for top jockeys, she just didn't know. What she did know was that it was the end of her long-held dream and perhaps she did need time to back off, mentally re-establish herself and re-align a realistic goal for her future.

The trainer's voice cut across her thoughts. 'Come and pick up your gear whenever you're ready. I'll have your P.45 and wages waiting for you in the office. Of course, I'll send your racecourse pass back to the Jockey Club and if I don't see you when you call in, thanks for working for me, Thalia. You've done a damn good job and if you ever need another job, phone me. Good luck.'

The click and subsequent dialling tone left Thalia staring at the phone in her hand. She lifted her gaze to the mirror on the wall in front of her. The pale reflection gazed back, grey eyes serious. 'And that, Thalia,' she murmured, watching her own lips move in the mirror, 'is that.'

★   ★   ★

It was over three weeks later that her mother, pronounced out of danger and beginning to mend, was sent home by ambulance. It was with very mixed feelings that Thalia and her three brothers grouped around their mother's bed, rejoicing that she was still alive, albeit very broken in body, yet definitely on the mend. But none of the four mentioned the loss of their father.

Thalia alone knew her mother's true feelings in that respect but she had sworn to keep her mother's secret and nothing would induce her to reveal it. However, the unsaid words hovered in the air above them all: Mother's come home, father is dead.

The three brothers, in typical male fashion, found it more than hard to express themselves emotionally through words — and didn't. But it was a palpable feeling in the air almost as though they were all on the same wavelength at that particular moment, tuning in and picking up what they were each thinking without it being uttered aloud.

It was Emma herself who voiced it. In a voice still very weak she said, 'My darlings, your father — he didn't suffer — when the car crashed, he was knocked unconscious and never came round. He died several hours later in hospital.'

The four of them stood as turned to stone, no-one courageous enough to break the silence. Emma continued. 'Just why it should have been your father that died, I don't know. He was the strong one . . . the survivor. I . . . the weak little woman.' Her voice trailed away and her eyelids closed.

Adam bent over, pressed her hand in his. 'Mother, rest now. It's all over. The funeral, all Father's affairs, all over, all sorted. We can't bring him back, we can only continue his work. The three of us,' he glanced at his two brothers, 'will now run the business. And Thalia will be living here to look after you.'

Emma opened her eyes, 'Racing?' she whispered, the query there as she looked across at Thalia.

Thalia forced a smile. 'On hold.'

'Later?' Emma's voice was very faint now but the query was there again.

Thalia thought of the inflexible time limit

to her racing dreams, mentally crossed her fingers and nodded. 'Yes, later.'

★ ★ ★

The next morning as Thalia closed the door after showing the District Nurse out, her thoughts picked up where they had left off in the conversation the previous evening. Later? Very much later, perhaps never. The full extent of her mother's injuries had only become apparent under the nurse's professional care and guidance that morning. It was clear they had all very much underestimated the length of time it was going to take before their mother was in any way fit again.

She flicked the switch on the electric kettle and slumped down onto the kitchen chair. There was no way to avoid it. She decided that when Adam, Ian and Simon were home tomorrow, Saturday, she would drive over to the racing stables at Waltham and collect her clothing and the few bits of racing gear that belonged to her, most particularly, her crash cap. She would then have to face the possible ordeal of meeting Dickson in the stable office as she collected her P.45 and the wages due to her.

It was hard enough to make a voluntary decision to give up a lifetime's dream but she knew that Dickson might try to persuade her to change her mind. Objectively, Thalia acknowledged she was a very capable stable lad and well up to the standard required for riding work. But the question really was could she continue improving and eventually become good enough to race on the courses?

It was questionable whether Dickson would take a chance on her improving and put in for a licence for her to ride as his apprentice stable jockey. But she knew the obstacle that perhaps he would find it convenient to hide behind and delay that choice was the fact that he already had Billy Renwick as his apprentice at Pegasus Stables. However, it was common knowledge that once Renwick had gained a couple of years' experience, it would be the natural thing, should he make the grade, for him to move away from a small stable like Dickson's and start to swim with the big boys at a larger racing establishment.

There was a loud hissing of steam and Thalia jumped up hurriedly as she realised the kettle was boiling. Laying a tray with cream, sugar and, for herself, honey, she topped two coffee mugs with scalding water and banged the kettle down with frustration — there were far too many if's.

She pulled down the shutter in her mind

on the possibilities. That's all they were, simply possibilities. Right now she needed to deal in hard facts. And the inescapable fact facing her was that her mother was badly injured, helpless and needing all the help that she, Thalia, could give.

She pushed open the door of her mother's bedroom, silently crossed the deep pile carpet and set down the tray on the bedside cabinet. The spoon settled in the sugar bowl and clinked against the china. Emma's eyelids opened and she smiled wanly at Thalia.

'Smells lovely. Are you joining me?'

Thalia nodded. 'I sure am. You're my number one priority.'

Emma's face relaxed at the words, visibly mirroring the soothing, cocooning effect those words had on her mentally and emotionally. As Thalia watched her mother's face became calm, peaceful, the shutter she had pulled down in her own mind, that still had a tiny get-out gap in it, finally clanged shut and she mentally attached the padlock. Her place was here now, at least for the foreseeable future.

'I think I'll tackle that coffee now.' Emma struggled to raise herself and Thalia packed the tri-cornered pillow behind her mother just as the nurse had done and eased Emma into a more comfortable position.

'Cream, Mother?'

'Yes, please, dear, and I'll be naughty. I'll have sugar, just a small one.'

'You can have two if you like. We've got to build you up, you know.'

'Yes, the sooner I'm well again, the sooner you can get on with your own life.'

Thalia spooned honey into her own coffee. The energy it gave had certainly helped during her working life in racing and the habit had stuck. She waved a dismissive hand and smiled at her mother. 'Just think, no more five-thirty starts.' Their smiles broadened.

'If you say so.' Emma looked sideways at her daughter. 'But you don't fool me. I'm your mother, remember?'

Thalia buried her face in the coffee mug to hide the wave of emotion which threatened to swamp her.

Emma lifted her own mug and took a sip of the deliciously hot coffee. 'Did you do what I asked you to, Thalia?'

Thalia lifted her head and looked at her mother with a puzzled expression. 'What? When . . . ?'

'At the hospital. I told you how things stood between your father and me. I asked you to buy a very large, thick notebook and a handful of pens.'

81

Thalia nodded slowly. 'Yes, I bought them. They're ready, but if you've changed your mind, now you're getting well again, I'll forget you ever said it. I realise you told me because you knew you might not pull through.'

'No.' Emma's voice was firm now, determined. She shook her head. 'I want you to become me as you write. It must be an honest account, however difficult a job that makes it. Anything less than the truth won't do.

'When I was at my lowest point in that hospital bed, I wanted to tell you the truth, Thalia. What I told you was only a fraction and I want to tell you the whole story. It may shock you, I hope it won't, but it has to be told.'

'Mother, you're getting well again now. As you say, you were at your lowest point and, possibly, you were going to die ... You wanted to clear your conscience. I understand that. Now it's different, it's changed. You're on the mend. If you wish, I'll just forget everything you said, completely clear it from my mind.'

Emma smiled lovingly at her daughter. 'What you don't understand, Thalia, is I *want* to tell you. I want you to write my story. I want you to make it readable, after all, you're the writer in the family, you've four books published. I know you write under a pseudonym and use your racing experience in your novels but you're a weaver of words.

'You once asked me if there was such a thing as perfect love, a love that lasts for a lifetime. Yes, there is — the true love between two soulmates. We cannot know if it is pure chance or destiny that causes us to meet. All I can say is, you will know when it happens. Love is the strongest thing in the world — it cannot be lost or severed — and when soulmates meet, there is a surety within our hearts we shall be together forever.

'I know this from personal experience.'

Thalia's face whitened and she looked incredulously at her mother. 'But you and Father — you weren't in love with him — you told me so . . . '

Emma reached for Thalia's hand and squeezed it gently. 'Be a good girl. Go and fetch the journal — my journal, as it will be. I can't write it myself but I can tell you what to write.' She released Thalia's hand and lay back against the pillow, energy spent, the blue veins in her eyelids standing out sharply against the fragile-looking, dead white skin.

Thalia pushed back the chair and blindly stumbled from the room. Just what her mother was going to reveal she had no idea, but she felt this was the verge of some momentous revelation that could possibly alter all their lives. She knew she didn't want to do this. She felt guilty at offering Emma a get-out by saying she could wipe it clean away from her memory. It wasn't to help her mother, it was to help herself. And her own selfishness fought inside with compassion for her mother's need to clear her conscience and be at peace.

Thalia stood on the landing, fists clenched hard, nails biting into palms and drew in deep, steadying breaths. It was no good. This was something she could not and should not shirk.

She had given up her life as it had been. This was life now — in the now — nursing and caring for her mother. Writing Emma's journal for her was just as much a task that needed to be done as bathing her, cleaning her teeth, brushing her hair, all the tiny, loving tasks that went into looking after that irreplaceable someone in your life who needs you — and only you.

Straightening her shoulders, Thalia marched off to her room, picked up the thick notebook with the hard covers and virgin white pages and the bundle of biros. Then hesitated. She sat down on her bed, turned over the first page and selecting one of the new pens, wrote in big black capitals:

JUNE 1978

EMMA'S JOURNAL

Then in smaller letters within brackets underneath:

(as dictated to me, her daughter, Thalia)

PART FOUR

1954

6

'Wendy, darling, I'm home.' Milo Kent closed the front door behind him and dropped his heavy, black, leather briefcase onto the oak chest. Tired after his consultancy duties at the hospital, he shrugged out of his jacket and draped it across the briefcase. Walking down the hall, he went into the lounge.

His wife, Wendy, was sitting in her wheelchair looking out through the wide patio window across the sweep of lawn and beyond to the shimmer of the lake. Her right hand raised as it always did when she heard his voice. In three strides he was by her side, kneeling down, gently taking hold of her hand and pressing it to his cheek. 'Hello, my darling. How've you been? A good day?' His professional eye ran over her features.

'Uhhu,' she said, affirming his words.

The usual engulfing tenderness and love rose in him at the sight of her face so hideously disfigured on one side. This half owed itself entirely to the expertise and care of the plastic surgeons. Her right eyelid now no longer drooped so completely over her sightless eye. The skin was no longer quite so puckered and drawn where it was stretched from the base of her nose across the cheekbone and up to her ear. A testament to the skill of the experts as they had implanted, reconstructed and grafted the right side of her face back into some semblance of normality. And nature had willingly co-operated and played her part in the healing.

In contrast, the other side of her face showed the former beauty she had been before suffering had cast a shadow over it — a shadow which, possibly, only Milo could distinguish. Her eyes were a beautiful dark iris blue, her lashes, thick and honey-coloured, and her hair, tumbling loose to her shoulders, completely hiding the wide, disfiguring scar along the side of her head, was just a shade deeper honey.

She lifted her face to his kiss. He was no longer surprised by the sweet, innocent, childish response her lips gave when they met his.

It had taken him a long time to acknowledge that Wendy, his Wendy, was now in stark reality, hardly more than a child. The accident had robbed her of full blooming womanhood and him of his wife.

He knew that by now, he ought to have come to terms with the results of that dreadful night — for his own sake he should come to terms with it — but he hadn't. And he hadn't really needed the psychotherapist's diagnosis of extreme personal guilt which blocked his own healing. Nothing could erase that guilt. It was his fault. No amount of counselling or help from the psychiatrist could alter the fact that he had virtually sent Wendy to a living death. The guilt was in no way mitigated by the fact that she herself was unaware of her own condition — seemed quite happy in her own small world.

Every time he saw her afresh at the end of his working day, it simply turned the handle of the merry-go-round in his brain. And it replayed with an astonishingly cruel clarity so that he was once again reliving the worst moment of his life when he returned home eight years ago.

It had been hot for days. The garden wilted, dry and parched under the heat of the August sun. His greenhouse temperature soared and topped an unbelievable 109, even with the vents fully open. It was one thing to grow orchids and reproduce a temperature warm enough for them but this was completely over the top. So that morning he had wedged open the greenhouse door before he'd left for the hospital.

On his way out to the garage, he'd stuck his head round the study door.

'Wendy? Would you mind, I've left the greenhouse door propped open. If it rains, could you close it for me, please?'

She'd looked up from the computer where she was already busy with an urgent translation needed for a medical journal.

'Yes, of course. I heard the early weather forecast and it gave thunderstorms later in the day for this area.'

'Probably be better if you take King George for his walk earlier rather than later, then he can settle in case we do get a big storm.'

At the mention of his name, the huge Great Dane lying under the desk lifted his head from his paws and surveyed Milo with a haughty, majestic stare.

'OK, old boy, you're certainly on the ball this morning, aren't you? Anyway, darling, must go. I'm going to be late. See you later.'

He had indeed seen her later. But she had not seen him.

The first storm broke around four in the afternoon. It had become increasingly oppressive as the afternoon drew on and Wendy had finally abandoned her work, and taken King George's short lead down from the hook on the back of the kitchen door. Together, they went out for a walk.

It was one of their usual walks along the

edge of the fields belonging to the nearby farm. The sky had an ominous bruised look over in the West that spread frighteningly quickly. As the sky darkened, it brought a threatening stillness with it. There had been just the odd half-dozen spots of rain, huge ones, as Wendy turned King George at the corner of the triangular field full of sugar-beet. 'We won't go any further,' she'd said, 'I don't fancy a good wetting.' And King George, with the finely tuned sixth sense that dogs have, had been only too ready to comply. Already his tail had drooped and he cocked an eye upward as a stiff little breeze sprang up and began shivering the narrow leaves on the ash tree growing in the hedgerow.

Within seconds, the wind gained strength and blew small dust clouds from the adjoining harvested field on the other side of the footpath. It gained in intensity, tugging at the telephone wires on their tall telegraph poles that traversed their way across the edge of the field and down into the village below. The wires bellied out and sang as the wind howled about them. There was a vivid flash of forked lightning and King George gave a deep, low whine of distress. Wendy refastened his lead.

'Come on, boy, we'll hurry it up and get

back. We'll take the short cut.'

By the time they reached home, the storm was only two or three miles away and had been joined by a second coming in from the North West. The sky was lit now by almost continuous flashes of lightning and the bellowing rolls of thunder were only seconds apart. The wind was now at its height, an intense screaming gale force that bent the trees and rattled the windows.

Wendy settled the big dog on his blanket under the kitchen table where he lay and shivered miserably. 'It will be over soon, boy.' She reached across, turned on the cold tap and filled the electric kettle to make a cup of tea. Glancing out of the kitchen window, she saw the first of the heavy rain had started, drops not just falling from the sky but being hurled from it, leaving big, wet blobs across the patio slabs outside.

The old elm tree, half-way down the garden bent and creaked as the merciless wind caught at the dead and decaying branches. Milo had been saying for months now he must get the tree lopped. Beyond the elm was Milo's greenhouse filled with his precious orchids and — oh, God! — the greenhouse door was still as he'd left it that morning, propped wide open. It was withstanding the full force of the storm because

Milo had jammed an enormous terracotta urn between the doorframe and the brick-work base of the greenhouse.

Wendy cast a glance upwards. The rain was certainly going to come down with a vengeance at any second. But she had promised. Flicking the switch on the electric kettle on her way out, she left the kitchen, closed the porch door so that King George couldn't follow her, and ran across the patio and down the garden path.

She'd gone perhaps half-way when the rain bucketed down, a wall of water being caught by the wild wind, seemingly throwing itself from sky to earth. Within seconds, Wendy's thin cotton dress and her long hair were saturated. No point now in turning back, she couldn't get any wetter. She ran on to the greenhouse.

The force of the wind held the door hard against the heavy urn and she struggled ineffectually to open it just an inch or two wider so that she could pull the urn out. Then came a sudden lull in the wind and the door came back quickly. Wendy seized the urn and tugged it, scraping, over the slabs clear of the door. She had just dragged it away when a screaming squall of wind and rain struck again, slamming the door shut.

But as the door closed, there was a jagged flash of fork lightning. One of the largest dead branches of the overhanging elm tree gave a hideous crack. It snapped away from the main trunk and plummeted downwards.

The heavy branch caught Wendy across the middle of her back, sending her plunging forwards. The right hand side of her head and face smashed against the hard, unyielding urn.

Milo found her there when he came home at six-thirty that evening. King George was howling behind the kitchen door, the electric kettle was still faintly warm from when it had boiled and switched itself off, and Wendy was still trapped beneath the fallen branch. It had been the worst moment of his entire life. He'd thought she was dead, so extensive were her injuries. The ambulance, with its usual efficiency, had been there within minutes.

That was eight years ago. The child just starting to grow inside Wendy's womb had died. Wendy had not — but neither had she fully recovered. At best, her condition could be described as a living death. The one saving grace in this, the brain damage itself protected her from memories of how she had once been.

Now Wendy was locked in an almost

childlike state, totally dependent on others for her needs in life.

She would never recover.

For Milo himself, his living death was the personal guilt that it was his fault. If he had had the tree lopped months before, as he should have done, it would not have happened. But it had happened. Now his burden lay on him every day of his life.

The one positive outcome was his decision to leave general practice and specialise as an Obstetrician. If he were to analyse himself objectively, he would probably have said that it was his way to make amends — to try to save lives. Particularly the lives of unborn babies — like the baby he and Wendy had lost.

As Milo left Wendy sitting in her wheelchair looking out at the lake that evening, he thought of the woman in Nightingale Ward who had wept with such extreme grief. What was her name? He didn't have to think. He knew her name. Somehow it was carved into his mind — Emma Wetherford. And when he had said to her, 'It's all right, I *do* understand,' she could not have known, had no way of knowing, just how true those words were.

He did understand — only too well.

Leaving Wendy and crossing the hall, Milo

tapped at the door on the left. 'Pearl?' A plump dark-haired woman, Wendy's personal nurse, opened it.

'Hello, Mr Kent.'

Pearl had been with the family now for the full eight years since the accident. She was treated as part of the family but always insisted on using his correct title.

'How're things today?'

It was her turn to look at his face with a professional, caring eye. She noted the tension lines around his eyes and the slight whitening of the skin denoting tiredness and strain.

'Just fine.' She smiled gently at him. 'You go and take time for yourself. The evening meal will be ready in about an hour. Wendy's just fine.'

'Thank you, Pearl. You're a godsend. You know that, don't you?'

'It's a pleasure to look after you both.'

He turned, picked up his case and jacket and went upstairs to shower.

★ ★ ★

Wendy had, of necessity, to stay downstairs on the level. To begin with he had considered moving out of their first floor bedroom, the double bed with its empty half mocking him every night when he climbed in. But he knew, in the end, he had to come to terms with the fact that Wendy would always remain more or less in the state she was in now, quite possibly through to old age.

They had given him a couple of options that he himself was well aware of after the final operation on her face.

'There're a couple of things you can do, Milo.' Gerald Seydon, Wendy's own doctor, had clasped him on the shoulder, looking him straight in the eye as he spoke. 'There are places, homes, for people with the same disability. She would be looked after twenty-four hours a day.' He'd nodded, mutely, even as the doctor was saying the words. 'Or, of course, you could employ a full-time nurse. In which case, Wendy could remain here at home.'

But Wendy's doctor had been wrong saying he had a choice. He didn't. He could not have lived with himself had he sent Wendy away. It was his fault she was in this condition, therefore, that made it his responsibility, his duty to care for her. And the sooner he accepted the situation, the sooner he could get on with the right sort of caring. He had to stop reaching back to the past — it was forever beyond his grasp.

So he mastered the choking spasm in his

throat, experienced every night when he climbed into that lonely, reproachful bed. Since their marriage, it had been such an oasis of warmth and love and bliss. Now it was all gone, forever. Yet despite the fact that it was years ago, he had never once looked at another woman or been physically stirred by the sight of one. His whole purpose now was to make amends through his own dedication looking after Wendy.

When he entered the bedroom, Milo kicked off his black shoes and padded across in his stocking feet to the window. It gave onto the same view that could be seen from downstairs in the lounge. But from this elevation, he could see beyond the lake and away over the hills to the skyline.

Always, after a long day at the hospital, he would come and gaze out at the wide expanse of peaceful countryside and the endless sky and allow his problems to shrink back into what they were — trivial — when viewed against the great scheme of life.

The view had been not the least of the deciding factors that had made him retain the house after the accident, at a time when he could not even bear to walk down the garden path past the neglected greenhouse.

Wendy had loved the house from the moment they had first seen it together a few months before their wedding day. She had declared it to be the only place for them. He had placed a deposit with the estate agent the next morning.

She would, even now in her limited state, feel familiar and at home here. He had done what he had thought the best thing for her. His personal feelings were to sell up, get away, but that would have been a very selfish action.

And so he had stayed, engaged the services of Pearl Blissett as personal nurse and lived each day on the day, looking neither forward nor back.

And it had worked — in a fashion — until today.

Turning from the window, he sat down heavily on the bed, swung his legs up, leaned back and relaxed full length. He didn't have to ask what was different about today. He knew. Today he had looked into the grief-stricken eyes of Emma Wetherford and she had looked back at him.

He had experienced what he could only describe to himself as a linking current which had passed between them, invisible yet undeniable. He had felt it, knew that she, too, had felt it.

However, at that moment mindful of their relationship as consultant and patient, he had stood up abruptly and stepped back — physically speaking. Inside it was already too late to back off — they had met.

This meeting was something he had unconsciously been waiting for since he was born. Or perhaps that wasn't quite true. He felt beyond any doubt they were meant to meet. It went beyond the five senses and touched the soul. He knew with absolute certainty, he had just discovered his true soulmate.

There was nothing in the least physical about it. It was on a far higher level than that but it was a linking and one that could not be denied. He had known when he looked into Emma's face as she lay in the hospital bed, that their future was inextricably woven together. Flight or fight would both be useless. They were each other's destiny.

It was as simple as that.

Milo heaved himself up off the bed and went to the bathroom. He turned the shower on very hot, stripped off each item of clothing, tossed it into the linen basket and stepped in.

Automatically, he reached for the soap and cleansed himself thoroughly and then stood with hands braced against the tiled wall and bent his head, letting the hot pounding needles beat against the back of his neck and the tautness of his shoulder muscles. He didn't know how long he stayed in that position, but he felt the tension drain from him, and run away down the plug-hole with the water.

However, it wasn't simply the tension of the day being released but tension from deep within which he hadn't realised he was holding on to.

Along with his bodily tensions, he felt his mind, his thoughts, his feelings, had all been set free from a long bondage and there was a beautiful magnificence about what had happened today.

He thanked God that he was privileged to know and to recognise his true soulmate. It was a humbling experience. The circumstances themselves were totally immaterial. His life from today would be different.

There was an up-rush of joy at what had been destined to happen. Fate, destiny, whatever, had brought them together. But alongside the joy was a deep sadness. Strangely, it elevated and enhanced the meeting because nothing was going to change. He was forever bound during this lifetime to look after Wendy — that was an inescapable fact.

And Emma Wetherford? She also was bound by her present set of material circumstances. He had checked her records: a married woman with three young children, her husband still alive — both living together. Milo knew that her circumstances too, were without doubt, unalterable.

But this was the day he had, unknowingly, waited for all these long thirty-nine years. Nothing could have prevented their meeting. It had happened. He acknowledged God's wisdom in bringing them together. It was as inevitable as both their lifestyles: a pre-ordained meeting at this time in their lives, within these particular sets of circumstances. Whatever the outcome, he would leave it all in God's hands.

7

Supper that night was very good — Succotash — Pearl really was an excellent cook. She always ate with Milo and Wendy. They took turns to assist the disabled woman, feeding her with a spoon, but even so there were frequent accidents. These were made light of, mostly turned into joke situations and, as usual, supper was a happy meal.

Afterwards, Pearl pushed Wendy in the wheelchair through to the lounge and switched on the television, said goodnight and retired to her own quarters.

'Just going through to my room, Mr Kent,' she called, sticking her head round the kitchen door.

Milo, clad in a full-length plastic apron, waved a soapy wooden spoon in the air. 'Thanks, Pearl. See you in the morning.'

She returned to her own room and Milo returned to the washing-up. It was a job he didn't mind. It gave him scope for thought and the view through the wide Georgian window to the East encompassed the same beautiful sweep of lawn from a slightly different angle.

He felt a sense of peace within that he had not known was missing until today. It was more a deep contentment that he felt through to the very core of himself. His part merely to follow through, do his best, and enjoy what came next.

So overwhelming was this feeling of contentment and assurance that he stepped aside briefly from it to question whether he was merely opting out, kidding himself this was happening. But his self-questioning, far from decrying the possibility, only reinforced his former feeling; at which point he gave up on the self-analysis, took up the tea towel and began to dry a stainless steel saucepan Pearl had used.

Whilst his hands were busy in mechanical mundane tasks, his thoughts turned again to Emma and he marvelled at the similarity of their situations. She was also learning the lesson of loss — they had both lost an unborn child.

Their individual grief was indeed very different but his had been offset by the shock and horror of Wendy's injuries. The loss of the child had been an added grief. Emma's loss, however, had been complete in itself — the child obviously had meant a very great deal to her.

But while they were both undertaking the

lesson of loss, surely what mattered would be how they both came to terms with it.

He himself had risen above it, had indeed taken a positive turn because of it, had studied, taken his exams and qualified as a Consultant Obstetrician.

He finished the washing-up, spread the tea towel out to dry, wriggled out of his apron and hung it up behind the pantry door.

Wendy was sitting in front of the television screen apparently totally absorbed. There was a very vocal advertisement on for dog food, showing some lively, glossy-coated collies bounding around, eagerly awaiting their meal.

Milo walked past the back of the wheelchair letting his hand brush against her honey-coloured hair, and dropped with a sigh of relief into the welcoming armchair next to her. She turned to smile at him and it tore at his heart, as always. The dreadful lopsided movement of her dear face, a grotesque caricature, that immediately brought him firmly back to earth, showed him where his duty still lay, and would to the end of his life.

He experienced the usual mix of emotion — the guilt, the sadness, a feeling of responsibility overall and yet underneath, as well, one which he could barely acknowledge, even to himself because it compounded the guilt — resentment. The unpleasant and unwelcome resentment was growing against all his wishes and his better nature.

Determinedly, he looked across at the television screen. The dogs were busily licking out their empty bowls, satisfaction in each wagging tail.

It crossed his mind, not for the first time, whether it would be a good idea if he were to get another dog for Wendy.

King George had died years ago. Great Danes were not a long-lived breed, their hearts in comparison to their bodies being extremely small, as was their capacity for exercise.

But he had seen the animation in her face as she watched the dogs on the television screen. He leaned across and took her hand.

'Darling.' She looked at him with her childlike gaze. 'Darling, would you like a dog?'

There, the words were out. He didn't know how Pearl would react — yet another responsibility being foisted upon her. He was under no illusion she would have to carry the brunt of it, he being away a great deal both at the hospital and also his private convalescent home.

The home was in Yorkshire on the coast at Sandsend, very near to Whitby. It had been opened not only for his patients' needs following their hospital treatment, but also from his acute awareness that he needed to be able to secure a substantial ongoing income in order to look after Wendy properly.

In addition to Pearl, he had two other nurses on whom he could call should Pearl be taken ill or go on much needed and frequent holidays.

Perhaps he really should have asked Pearl her opinion first but it was too late now. He'd made the offer. He hadn't planned to offer Wendy the chance of getting a dog — it was a spur of the moment impulse, one he desperately hoped he would not have to withdraw.

Wendy's smile had spread, hideously contorting her face even more and she nodded her head, 'Uugh, uugh, uugh.'

Shame pricked him keenly. What he had offered her was so very little for all that she had lost because of him. Too late now for misgivings. In her childlike way, she would expect and anticipate its arrival.

'Of course, my darling, I'll have to have a word with Pearl because she will help you to look after the new dog, won't she?'

Wendy nodded vigorously.

'We shall have to ask her what breed of dog she'd prefer. After all, she will be here all day looking after it. It's possible that she wouldn't want a large dog, like King George.'

The smile died instantly from her face and the shadowed look appeared again. Milo could have kicked himself. He carried on hurriedly, 'But we will see what Pearl thinks.'

Wendy pointed to a photograph on the mantlepiece showing their Great Dane dog. Milo went over and picked it up, passing it to her. She hugged it close.

'Tomorrow, my sweet, tomorrow.' He patted her hand. 'I'll have a word with Pearl. Everything will be all right. Leave it to me.' Her smile reappeared.

Music from the television set announced the start of a nature programme and a picture of a giant panda came on the screen. Instantly, Wendy's attention was caught. Holding her hand, Milo sighed gently, leaned back and relaxed. Wendy watched the programme, enraptured.

At half-past nine, Milo switched off the set and pushed her wheelchair through to the modified bathroom adjoining her bedroom. He ran hot water into the bath and spread the rubber bathmat out.

'Which one tonight, Wendy?' He showed her an array of coloured perfumed foam baths.

With childish pleasure, she giggled and jabbed a finger towards a pink one.

He slipped off her clothes quickly and

110

ignored the hoist, picking up her slight form and depositing her gently down into the warm bath water. Taking a flannel from the bath-rack, he began soaping her back, neck and arms while she splashed and wriggled her toes happily in the bubbles. He moved forward and tenderly washed her chest and small breasts.

This was the part where previously he'd desperately needed to remind himself he was a doctor. Although Wendy was officially his wife, morally, she was merely entrusted to his care.

But it had been a long time since performing this loving duty for her had stimulated him physically. Now, he made a joke of it, splashing her back with warm water as she was splashing him.

Then wrapping the huge, warm towel around her body, he lifted her, wriggling and giggling from the bath, and walked through to the bedroom. He sat in the wooden rocking chair beside the bed cuddling her gently to him, rocking softly back and forth whilst the thick towel absorbed the wetness from her body.

Wendy put her arms around his neck and snuggled her face under his chin. His heart melted as it always did at the childlike trust. No way would he ever betray her. Finally, he slipped on her nightie, folded back the sheet and tucked her up gently in bed. 'Goodnight, Wendy, my darling.' He bent over and kissed her cheek, felt the contrast between her soft skin and the puckered coarseness of the raised ridge of the scar itself. 'Sweet dreams, my love, I'll see you in the morning.' And then he turned out the light.

The next morning, Milo was up a few minutes before his normal time and, going down to the kitchen, found Pearl already preparing breakfast.

'Morning, Pearl.'

'Good morning, Mr Kent. Looks like we're going to have another beautiful day.' He looked across to the lake where the swifts were dipping and swooping across the surface of the water.

'Yes, the birds are already out in force.'

'Maybe they've heard about the early bird and the worm.' Pearl deftly cut some slices from the wholemeal loaf.

'I have something to ask you, Pearl.'

'Oh? That sounds ominous.' She slid two slices into the toaster and turned to look enquiringly at him.

'I didn't really intend to say it last night, but somehow it slipped out. Wendy was engrossed in watching some dogs in an advert on the television and she looked . . . '

'Alive?' Pearl glanced sideways at him.

'Yes, that's exactly it. She looked alive.'

Pearl nodded and continued putting bread into the toaster.

'Of course, you know what I'm going to say, don't you?'

'You asked her if she would like a dog.' It was a statement.

Milo laughed. 'You're a witch.'

Pearl grinned. 'Thank you very much.'

'Oh, in the nicest possible way.'

'What was Wendy's reaction?' Pearl was serious now.

'What do you think?'

'So?'

'So, what I thought immediately was, what a bloody fool I am.'

'How come?'

'Look.' He spread his hands flat on the kitchen table. 'You're here, thank God you're here, to look after us. But with me working away a great deal, the whole business of looking after a dog would fall on you. I should have consulted you first, before saying anything at all to Wendy. I realise that but it's too late now, I've already said it. The best thing I can do to make amends is to ask you now. Please would *you* mind if we do have a dog? It's not for me I'm asking, it's for her.'

'Mr Kent,' Pearl set down the milk jug with

an unsteady hand, 'she has so very, very little in her life. How could I possibly say no to something that I'm sure would bring her immense pleasure? It wasn't my place to suggest it to you, but I'm so very glad you've brought up the subject. I wouldn't mind in the slightest, in fact, I'd be delighted.'

A weight he hadn't known was there lifted from Milo's shoulders and he gave her a quick hug. 'If ever you leave us, I don't know what the hell I shall do. If that sounds extremely selfish, it is. If you ever do want to leave us, please forget I ever said that.'

'Don't worry,' Pearl laughed, 'I'm more than happy to be here.'

'Right. So, Madam, you have the honour of deciding which breed of dog we should bring into the home. I've already told Wendy that it's your decision. It is the one clarifying remark I made after offering her a dog.'

'How kind.' A pink flush spread over Pearl's plump cheeks. 'Well, I don't know . . . it's taken me by surprise . . . '

'Think about it, let me know tonight.'

She nodded, 'I will. I think we'll have a game, Wendy and I, during the day while you're away. I'll draw her some pictures or we'll look at some pictures of dogs and we'll see what we can agree upon.' Milo took both her hands in his.

'Bless you.' And he meant it.

The thought went through his mind, God supplies every need, even before you ask Him.

Could Pearl be one of these predestined people who came into his life right at the point when he needed them? In which case, his thoughts ran on further, was this the point in his life when he needed Emma Wetherford?

8

Milo drove into the hospital in high spirits. He loved his work and looked forward to the start of each day to check how his patients were progressing, to meet the challenge that this day's new patients would bring to him and just how he could use his skill to help them. He found himself humming happily as he swung the car into his allocated parking space.

When Clinic was over and the time came to do the ward round on Nightingale, he experienced an even greater lift of spirit. In eager anticipation, he pushed open the swing doors. Casting a swift glance around the ward, his eyes met Emma's for the briefest of moments — but even that sent his pulses racing. He found it difficult to focus his mind on the particular patient in each bed during his slow assessment visit down the ward and yet every one of his patients was still important. It was very disconcerting.

He tried very hard to be his normal self but he could detect the almost imperceptible sidelong glances that the nurses directed towards him when they thought he wasn't looking. Was his ebullient air so apparent? Or was he just being oversensitive?

He approached Emma Wetherford's bed with a frisson of excitement coursing through his entire body.

As he struggled to hold down this excitement, he was momentarily unprepared for the sight of tears trickling down Emma's face.

Immediately, his professionalism snapped into place. 'Not still crying, surely?' It wasn't said harshly but it was said firmly. As a consultant, he knew this was the correct approach but part of him longed to drop on his knees beside the hospital bed and hold that woman in caring, tender arms. Just hold her — until she gained the strength herself to restart on her personal pathway of healing. Instead he simply smiled and let a little of the warmth he was feeling show through his eyes. He knew instantly that she had picked up on the warmth and found comfort in it.

He forced himself to take the first step away from her that led on to the next patient in his charge. The light within him became damped down, muted, and before he had finished attending his last patient, he was already longing for an opportunity to return to her bedside again.

Had it been a colleague in this situation,

and they had come to him for advice on how to handle it, he would, of course, have told them to put an immediate end to all such thoughts. If possible, to delegate one of the housemen or failing that, to cut to the barest minimum the time spent in the woman's presence. It was complete madness to allow the feelings to blossom. That's what he would have told a colleague. What he told himself was all these things — and none of them had the slightest effect.

And whenever he thought of her, the glorious sensation inside him blossomed like a rose opening to the June sunshine. Where it would end, God alone knew. Certainly, Milo had not the slightest idea.

All he knew was that he was being swept away by the current in a surging, boiling torrent of white-crested water, as helpless as a drowning kitten.

For the rest of the day Milo buried himself in his work — according each of his patients equal consideration. Only by total concentration was he able to blot out all thoughts of Emma.

By the time he came out of the main doors and crossed the car park to his vehicle, he knew himself to be a tired man but it was a tiredness that was mixed with satisfaction. He was in the right place doing the right job. Not

118

many men could say that. And he drove home contentedly with a quiet sense of achievement.

He was looking forward to seeing Wendy. He wondered if Pearl would have managed to guess the right breed of dog which would fit in with their lifestyle and bring some happiness into Wendy's life. If anyone could, Pearl certainly could. She was a gem by name and by nature. He had to remind himself at times that he must not put on her more than he should.

Parking the car, he went in. 'Wendy, darling, I'm home.' Following the usual routine, he took his place beside her wheelchair, pressing her palm against his cheek. Pearl discreetly allowed him a few minutes before she tapped on the door and came in. He smiled up at her. 'How're things?'

'Fine, Mr Kent. Look what we've achieved today.' She held out a sketchpad to him. Several pages were filled with drawings, not expertly done admittedly, but certainly discernible as specific breeds of dogs.

Milo squeezed Wendy's hand. 'And have you picked one, my love?'

Wendy nodded vigorously. 'Uugh, uugh, uugh.'

'You show me.' He spread the sketchpad on

her knee and released her hand. Very slowly, he turned each page, looking up at her encouragingly with each new breed of dog displayed. She giggled, shaking her head, entering into the spirit of the game until he turned one of the pages and she immediately jabbed a finger forwards.

'Uugh,' she cried.

He twisted his head round to see which one it was. Then he looked up at Pearl and said, 'Predictable, so predictable.'

'Yes, indeed.'

'And are you sure you can manage?'

'Quite sure.' Pearl put a hand on Wendy's head and smoothed down a lock of hair that had displaced itself by the violent shaking. 'I think the sooner we get one the better.'

'Perhaps a young dog rather than a pup might be the better choice.' Milo pursed his lips. 'Shall we say one that's already been house-trained and obeys the basic com-mands?'

'Very well,' Pearl laughed. 'You could be right.'

Milo cupped his hand under Wendy's chin and lifted her face. 'And have you two girls thought of a name yet?'

'Not yet,' Pearl replied. 'It's a bit like chocolate cake, really,' she smiled, 'very rich if you eat it all at once, if you follow my drift.'

'Aah, ha,' Milo nodded. 'Well, I'll leave it to you. I'm off to get a shower.'

'See you in about an hour,' said Pearl.

He left both women poring over the drawing of a Great Dane.

★ ★ ★

Two days later, he grasped the nettle. There was no valid reason for Emma Wetherford to remain in hospital any longer. It was time for her discharge back home. In his rooms at the hospital, Milo suppressed the resentment within him at the thought of handing Emma a pass out of the bed, the hospital — his life.

'Usual discharge letter, Susan, please. Send to Doctor Cordley, the G.P. at Bingham, regarding his patient, Emma Wetherford. Take the details from the file. Diary it for a home visit follow-up by myself in a month's time, and two or three days prior to that, send a letter giving Mrs Wetherford advance notice of that visit. Thank you.'

It was done. The only way he could back out now was if she had an unexpected relapse, and she wouldn't, he was sure of it. Her bodily health was progressing nicely, what her mental state was, well . . . that was something else.

The time for ward visit slowly approached

121

and the now familiar rise of expectation within him was gaining in strength with each day that went past. Logic told him that perhaps it was a good thing she would be discharged today. But that was logic.

The whole of his being screamed out in protest. He needed to see her, speak to her, albeit even briefly. The whole of his life now centred around this — everything else seemed simply the back-cloth to that one spotlight in the day.

However much he fought against it, he might just as well have tried to stem a breach in a dam with his finger. It was useless to flee from or to fight against, he'd been swept over the rapids. The only thing to do now was allow them to flow — and see where they led.

How it affected Emma he had no idea. But if the emotion was so strong within him, he could only surmise that it was a reciprocated feeling and that she in her turn would be geared each day to the moment he approached her. Or was he being unbelievably big-headed? It was a question he'd asked himself a hundred times.

At eleven o'clock he preceded the nurses through the swing doors of Nightingale Ward. He paused and let his gaze run down the length of the ward. As he looked at Emma's bed, she was already sitting up and looking towards them. Even from that distance, her eyes met his and he instantly felt that indescribable mystical current — a chemical reaction linking them.

He switched his gaze back, knowing he could not veil the exquisite surging joy with which her look had filled him. The nurses grouped themselves around the foot of the first bed. Once more, he drew the cloak of professionalism firmly about him, and concentrated on his first patient. Studying notes, querying states of well-being, issuing or amending instructions to staff, he slowly made his way down, patient by patient, bed by bed.

Until it was Emma's turn. He studied the notes at the foot of her bed, absorbing, understanding, updating himself on her physical progress. Finally, he raised his eyes and looked at her.

The unmistakable current joined them as firmly as a physical union. And he read in her eyes what he was feeling within himself, knew that the question he had asked himself a hundred times had, at that point, been answered.

'I have some very good news for you, Mrs Wetherford.' Emma looked at him in anticipation. 'You've made extremely good progress and I consider that you are well enough to be discharged. You may go home today.' Although the words left him with a feeling of cold numbness in his stomach, he smiled at her.

'That's very good news,' she smiled back. 'Thank you, Mr Kent.'

'I shall, of course, be writing to your own doctor. I want you to continue with the iron tablets. But apart from that, plenty of rest, nourishing food, get outside and have lots of good fresh air. It works wonders.' He smiled at her — she smiled back — and the whole of the hospital ward was non-existent for both of them.

'Thank you for all you've done. I'll certainly take your advice,' she murmured.

He nodded. 'Any problems, do contact your own G.P. I shall, of course, be making a home visit in about four weeks to make sure you're progressing satisfactorily.'

'You will?'

'Yes, it's normal practice. I'll have my secretary send you a letter a day or two before to confirm that the day and time are convenient to yourself.'

'Thank you.'

'If you do have any problems, I could offer you a place at my private convalescent home. It would mean a journey up to Yorkshire, but we'll see — it's entirely up to you and there may be no need. But there is always that option, should you require it.'

'I'm sure I shall be perfectly all right, but thank you, anyway.'

He transferred the notes to his left hand, went a little closer to the side of her bed and held out his right hand. 'I do wish you the very best.'

Her eyes locked with his as she in turn reached out and put a slim hand into his. A charge of energy zipped between them, unseen, unnoticed by everyone else. It conveyed everything they were feeling and each understood that soundless message.

* * *

Milo drove home from the hospital that evening with a weight of depression upon him which he would not have believed possible. There was a hollow emptiness inside and he felt as though a sizeable part of his body had been amputated. He wondered how Emma was coping with what must be similar emotions.

The whole relationship had been perfectly proper as between Consultant and patient and yet he knew that it would not end here, could not end here. He had to see Emma again.

He did not feel in the least like going home. Although he knew it was absurd and unrealistic, he had to fight to stop his hands turning the wheel of the Daimler and going to see where it was Emma lived. He knew the address by heart. Buttery Lane, Alney.

Wendy and he lived about twenty miles south in Leicestershire. No distance for a powerful car. He fought down the urge to go and find the village, simply drive past and look at the house where she now was.

On the steering wheel, his knuckles showed white. He hadn't realised the amount of willpower he was having to use to stop himself from turning that wheel.

Resolutely, Milo clenched his jaw, put his foot down hard and drove home.

9

The alarm clock rang at seven. In the half-light, I peered at the clock face. Since coming out of hospital, I hadn't bothered setting the alarm. There had been no need. The summer holidays stretched in front and the boys were not bound by time. That meant neither was I. Muzzily, I put out a hand and stopped the alarm. I began to come round. The first day of school term. My spirits plummeted instantly. Today I had to take the twins back to school for the start of the new term.

Adam had returned to boarding school at the end of last week. Somehow, this hadn't had the same effect upon me as the thought of losing the twins today. Adam was approaching his ninth birthday and had already acquired a veneer of independence undoubtedly brought about by his sojourn at boarding school. I had mentally come to terms a long while ago with it that most of the time he would be apart from me.

But the twins were only five, still dependant, and it brought everything back with a rush. The whole reason why I'd wanted so very much to become pregnant again and hopefully to have a daughter. The twins beginning at the village school after Easter had been a major catalyst in my life.

When Dr. Cordley had shaken my hand warmly in the surgery such a few short weeks ago, I had been convinced that life would now, not only be bearable, but also would hold the possibility of fulfilment and happiness again.

When I had returned from hospital after losing my precious baby, the only thing which supported me was my three boys who were all at home from school for the summer holidays.

I had had to put on a brave front concealing as much as possible of what I really felt inside. I had certainly managed to during the day, but when the children had gone to bed I, too, had said goodnight to Charles, taken a long, warm, soothing bath and gone to my own single bed in the guest room.

Charles had, as I'd thought, accepted unquestioningly my reason behind this — more peace and quiet, more rest. In fact, he didn't seem to be in the slightest bit bothered that I, as his wife, was no longer sharing his bed.

I had spent numb, dry-eyed, grief-filled

nights in that lonely bed, mourning the loss of my unborn child, usually only falling asleep from exhaustion in the early hours to awaken with relief from horrible, torturing nightmares, heavy-eyed and unrefreshed.

During the day, the exuberant, natural high spirits of the twins had carried me along and I had been extremely careful not to let the grief show whilst I was with them. Now, today, in only an hour's time, I would be taking them to school, then returning to that most awful of places, an empty, childless house. But first, I had to get myself going and get them ready for school. I flung back the bedclothes.

★ ★ ★

I stood together with the rest of the young mothers clustered round the school gates waving, smiling, watching our offspring walk away — little plump calves rising from sparkling white socks and conker-bright polished new sandals marching sturdily forward, satchels bumping against bottoms. Getting on with their lives. As they entered the school, the twins clutched each other's hand.

I turned blindly away, blinking rapidly to stem my hot tears. It was no good. As they had walked on, so must I. I had to put everything behind me now and look to the future. The future was what mattered now, the future. I found myself repeating it as I walked home.

Taking out my key, I opened the front door. Charles had already left for business before I had taken the twins to school. The unmistakable atmosphere of an empty house overflowed into the hall, over the doorstep and over me.

I took a deep breath and went in. On the doormat lay a foolscap envelope. I closed the door and picked up the letter, taking it through to the kitchen. It was printed along the top with the words 'Nottingham Women's Hospital'.

My fingers began to shake as I held it and my thoughts flew back to those few seconds when I had last seen Mr Milo Kent, my obstetric consultant. I remembered what he had said and glanced up at the calendar on the wall. Yes, it was three weeks since I had been discharged. This, then, must be the letter notifying me of the day and time he was going to come and visit me.

I suddenly felt giddy and sat down on the kitchen chair. Ripping open the envelope, I drew out the single sheet of paper. Yes, it was confirmation of his visit, Thursday, ninth

September, 1954. And as I looked at the date, in my mind's eye, I could see him, with his curly, fair hair, finely planed intelligent face and his hazel eyes slowly crinkling at the corners and filled with genuine warmth.

Unsteadily, I rose to my feet, took a red biro from the side of the phone and drew a red circle on the calendar around the ninth.

★ ★ ★

'What's important about the ninth of September?' Charles' voice drifted through the open serving hatch from the kitchen as I was laying the dining table for the evening meal. I placed the last fish knife on the tablecloth and went back to the kitchen.

'I had a letter this morning, Charles, from the consultant, Mr Kent. He's coming to see me on a home visit.'

'Whatever for?' His eyebrows drew together in a frown.

'He's coming to assess my recovery and if need be, to offer me the opportunity of a stay at his convalescent home in Yorkshire.'

Charles' frown deepened to a scowl. 'What on earth for? It's a complete waste of the man's time coming here. You've made a full recovery.' He let go of the page of the calendar, flicked it contemptuously with his

131

fingernail and went back to the lounge.

I stood, fists clenched, seething inside. Just how did Charles know I'd made a full recovery? We had not had a conversation apart from the odd sentence here and there since I'd been discharged from the hospital. There had been no close one-to-one talks in bed, no outings. With a determined effort, I unclenched my hands and took several deep breaths. Whatever level of healing I'd achieved, it was through my own efforts.

Mr Kent's suggestion whilst I'd been in hospital of my having a chat with Mrs Huggett had indeed been a turning point in my getting well. It had stopped me turning inwards on myself, feeding on my own depression, to think of someone else's misery. But it had been no easy task. And there had been several times since I'd been home when I could have lain down and simply never got up again, the sheer effort of carrying on life almost too much and the thought of an empty future completely untenable. But those times I had concentrated upon the twins and Adam and their needs — not my own. It had helped. What I did not need was Charles casually glossing over the depth of the desolation that I was still fighting desperately to overcome.

On the morning of the ninth September

the day had started with heavy rain pouring down. I had risen early, bathed and dressed and taken the twins to school as normal. When I returned home, the day was regretting its miserable start and already the sun was beginning to dry the pavements.

I went up to the bedroom, stripped off my customary slacks and shirt, opened the wardrobe door and ran a critical eye along the rail. Finally, I chose a lemon coloured summer dress with square neckline. Its image was totally in keeping with my, for once, optimistic mood.

Promptly at eleven o'clock the front door bell rang. Although I had been expecting it, my heart now began to pound and I felt panic sweep over me. Don't be ridiculous, I chided myself, this is your consultant, remember? But all I could remember was the warmth of his hazel eyes as he had seemed to link in with my own emotions.

I cast a quick glance in the hall mirror as I passed and patted my hair into shape. Then I opened the door. Milo Kent stood there, exactly as I had seen him in my mind's eye, wearing a charcoal-grey suit, white shirt and maroon tie. For a long moment we stood there and looked at each other.

'May I come in?'

Stupidly, tongue-tied, I nodded.

'You did receive the letter from my secretary telling you I was calling today?'

'Yes, yes, I did. Won't you go through, have a seat . . . ' I showed him into the lounge. 'Excuse me, I'll just make some coffee.'

'Fine,' he said smiling, 'I'd love one.'

I'd laid the tray ready and only needed to boil the kettle. As I carried the tray through, he turned round from where he stood admiring a reproduction Stubbs painting.

'My young half-brother's horse mad,' he said breaking the ice, as I fumbled to set the tray down without spilling the cream. 'He swears he's going to earn his living working with horses.'

'Well, I suppose it makes a change from wanting to be a train driver.' I returned his smile. I appreciated his sauve expertise in overcoming a difficult moment. 'How do you like your coffee?'

'I don't really mind.' I looked at him uncertainly, he was still smiling. 'I'm surrounded by well-intentioned ladies who know exactly how I prefer coffee. I'd like you to choose for me this time.'

I felt once again as I had felt at my first job at the golf club — a gauche, inexperienced girl confronted by a self-assured man of the world who was making me feel someone special. But I was not. And the memory of

134

how Charles had completely taken over and dominated me brought a rise of antipathy. 'I'd rather you just tell me, please,' I said abruptly.

His eyebrows rose a fraction. 'OK, black, no sugar.'

I handed him the cup. Poured myself one and defiantly adding a liberal spoonful of Demerara, I stirred it vigorously, trying to understand my racing feelings.

This man stirred me as no other had ever been able to do, not even Charles. But the feeling he generated within me was far more frightening. I would have described it more as exhilaration, anticipation. What did frighten me was my reaction to this feeling.

Milo Kent took a sip of the hot coffee and returned the cup back to the saucer. 'Now, I would like you to tell me, please, how you've been since your discharge from hospital.' He leaned back in the chair and folded his hands.

To gain time, I stood up, walked to the window and began sipping my own drink. He didn't say a word but gave me the space to gather my own thoughts.

'I've been managing . . . ' I took another sip. 'I've had to make the effort because of the summer holidays and my three sons. They need me, you see.' Still he didn't say anything, and I blundered on. 'Of course, my husband, Charles, thinks all this is a complete waste of time, your visiting. He told me so. Said I was completely well again now.'

'And what do you say? Are you completely well?' His voice was low, gentle.

I tried, my God, I tried, not to let those pathetic tears escape from under my tightly squeezed eyelids. But it was no good, I couldn't stop them. I felt them trickle down my cheeks. Biting hard on my lower lip, I stayed with my back to him, ostensibly looking out through the window. Finally, I managed to mumble, 'No, at least . . . I don't think I am.'

'Would you like to explain any further?'

I swung round then, placed the cup and saucer on the coffee table. 'He doesn't know, doesn't care,' I burst out. 'He assumes I'm all right.'

Milo Kent sat, his face impassive, watching me. I began to walk up and down the carpet. 'I haven't slept with him. I moved straight into the guest room when I came back from the hospital. I can't bear the thought of him near me. Much less sleep with him, be a wife to him.'

He bent his head and appeared to inspect his fingernails. 'Do you think this will get better, as you progress with getting well?'

'No!' I burst out vehemently, 'I do not.'

136

He changed tack suddenly. 'I understand you took my advice and went to have a word with Mrs Huggett whilst you were on the ward. I thought she had told you she could not have any children — that in fact, she had none at all.'

I nodded. 'It was the right thing for you to tell me to do. That was the turning point against going deeper into my own depression. It pulled me up short.'

He smiled briefly. 'Good. However, don't you think that given your circumstances, perhaps it might be the answer if you were to try for another child?' His gaze now was very direct. I met his eyes unflinchingly.

'It would be the last thing on earth I want to do.'

'Have you been to see your own doctor?'

'No.'

'Perhaps you ought to consider doing so, and maybe, starting a course of anti-depressants.'

I shook my head. 'When Dr Cordley told me I was pregnant, that was the point when I stopped having to take sleeping tablets.'

He looked at me shrewdly. 'Yes, I know. It's in your notes. But antidepressants are different from sleeping tablets.' I waited. Eventually, when the silence had stretched for longer than was comfortable he said, 'Mrs

137

Wetherford, what do *you* want to do?'

I turned and looked at him. That frisson of current sparked between us again and I knew very clearly what I wanted. I suspected beneath the professional manner we were back to basics here — a man and a woman and an almighty attraction. It was useless to deny. I knew he was also feeling the same without having to say anything. But he was leaving it up to me. 'I would like to take up your offer, Mr Kent, and spend a short time at your convalescent home.'

He dropped his gaze and looked at his hands again, pursing his lips. 'I thought you'd say that,' he murmured softly.

I began to tremble a little, shaken by the forwardness of my own words, but I did not want to retract. The rights and the wrongs simply did not enter into it. I had known inside all along that I was heading towards an unseen destiny — one not only exciting but potentially dangerous. It was like being propelled forward down a very steep hill without brakes. And how marvellous it felt, at that moment, to be alive.

10

It was arranged I should go to the convalescent home the second week in October. This would allow for a full week's stay before I needed to come home at the start of the twins' half-term holiday.

Charles, predictably, was extremely annoyed. 'Good God, woman. You don't need to go there. You're as well as you ever were.'

Far from sowing doubts in my mind, his words irritated me intensely and made me more determined that I should go.

'We've just had to manage without you only four weeks ago, and now you'll be gone again.'

I felt as though he had slapped me across the face.

'Charles,' I said in a very controlled, low voice, 'I was taken into hospital because of your child.' A bitchy part of me deliberately emphasised that it was his fault. It was unfair, but he did not seem to notice.

'Oh come now,' he said, 'you were the one that wanted the child, not I.'

I was trembling with temper now. 'Yours, mine, for God's sake! I am going to the convalescent home whether you like it or not.'

He laughed nastily and narrowed his eyes. 'And I suppose,' he said, 'you'll expect me to pay for it.'

In the days that followed, we barely spoke to each other. I made my own arrangements, deciding that I would travel up by train to Scarborough and from there by bus to Horizon House convalescent home at Sands-end.

* * *

On the morning I was due to leave, I sought Charles out in the bathroom. I did not want the twins overhearing what could be either a reconciliation or a confrontation. 'I've pinned the convalescent home telephone number up on the cork board in the kitchen. If there are any emergencies or if you just . . . want to speak to me, that's where you can reach me . . . ' My voice trailed away as he continued to concentrate on his shaving. His eyes swivelled sideways in the mirror as he looked at me indirectly.

'I don't expect I shall need to,' he said stiffly.

'Well, let's hope not,' I said. 'I wouldn't like to be away from home if I were needed.'

'You're not. We can manage perfectly well.

We've had to before, don't forget.'

I had held out an olive branch but I felt my grip on it begin to slip. 'Charles, I didn't invoke my miscarriage. It was the last thing, the very last thing, in this world I wanted to happen.'

'No,' he agreed grudgingly, 'I don't suppose you did. But it still didn't alter the fact you weren't here. And now we've got to cope again.'

There was a petulant, 'poor me' note in his voice and I had to try very hard to fight down the irritation I felt. I took a firmer grip on the olive branch. 'I shall be back at the end of a week, it's not that long. I feel I must go, Charles. I need to get some space, some perspective upon life. I simply don't seem able to carry on at the moment.'

He didn't answer me but carried on shaving. I was floundering now and knew it. A one-sided olive branch really wasn't going to save anything. It needed a hand at both ends. 'When I come back,' I said, trying not to part on these terms which had already created a nasty taste in my mouth, 'it will be the twins' half-term holiday. Could we take them away for a few days, as a family?'

He looked at me scornfully. 'Don't be stupid, Emma. What about the business?' The

141

olive branch slipped a little further from my grasp.

'Well, couldn't it manage without you just for a short time? I'm sure one of the managers would take over any necessary decision making.'

'Oh yes,' he said sarcastically, 'they're going to take my place are they, on the golf course . . . sign cheques and documents? Be your age.' His remarks stung but I still clung stubbornly to the last inch of that slippery twig.

'Possibly a long weekend then, Charles, what do you say to that?'

He grunted. 'I'd have to think about it.'

At this slim opening, my hopes rose. 'Do try, Charles. It would be very good for all of us to be together as a family.'

'Stop haranguing me, Emma. I've told you, I'll think about it.'

And then he went and spoilt it by adding, 'However, if I were you, I wouldn't hold my breath.' He dropped the razor with a decisive splash into the handbasin.

I turned and went back downstairs to the kitchen more confused than ever. I picked up the kettle and filled it — the essential British stand-by for every emotional dilemma — and made a pot of tea.

The previous night I had spent most of the

time tossing and turning in that lonely single bed knowing that I would have to be the first one to make a move to smooth things over. I didn't want all this discord in the air. If I could feel it then the twins, as sensitive children, would surely also pick it up and it was not in their best interests. Children needed a loving, stable atmosphere to grow up in. But still, I had tried. If Charles wouldn't meet me halfway or even partway, there was nothing else I could do.

At his usual time, Charles picked up his briefcase, kissed the twins goodbye and walked out the front door.

'Charles? Are you going now?'

'Of course I am,' he said with disdain, 'I always leave for business at this time.' And he walked out to where the car was parked.

I stood and watched the curl of vapour from the exhaust as it accelerated away down the drive. So that was that. No goodbye said, no well-wishing. The olive branch slipped completely from my grasp and fell to the floor. Forgetting my resolve to try and stabilise the atmosphere within the home for the sake of the boys, I banged the front door hard releasing at least a little of the resentment which was roaring through me.

★ ★ ★

It was a bad moment when I said goodbye to the twins at the school gates. I kissed them soundly, put an arm around each and the three of us clung together.

'Don't want you to go, Mummy,' Ian pouted.

'Don't go, Mummy,' echoed Simon, sticking a thumb into his mouth, something he hadn't done for months.

It took all I had to jolly them along, saying lightly, 'Mummy will be home again soon, darlings, be good boys for Daddy.' Reluctantly — guiltily — I released them whereupon they immediately held hands as they trailed up the school drive, turning now and again to wave half-heartedly. I deliberately slapped on a broad smile and waved back enthusiastically until they had gone through the doors. Immediately they disappeared, so did my smile.

Miserably, I walked home, the thought of whether I was doing the right thing in going away tumbling over and over in my mind as it had done most of the previous night. But it was all fixed now, far too late to change the arrangements.

There was a place ready and waiting for me at the convalescent home. Milo Kent would be there, too. I felt as though I was being stretched like a piece of elastic. But the

144

outcome was already settled and at the core of my being, I was already in Yorkshire with him.

★ ★ ★

I prowled up and down the hall, checking my watch every few seconds waiting for the peep on the horn outside to tell me the taxi had arrived.

When, finally, the horn sounded, I almost fell over myself in my urgency to pick up suitcase and handbag. With trembling fingers, I locked the front door behind me and scrambled into the taxi.

'Newark station?' The driver twisted his head round.

'Yes, please.'

'Which one?'

'Oh, Northgate, please.'

It was draughty on the platform. A stray pigeon pecked listlessly, its feathers ruffled by the wind. I placed my suitcase on the empty seat but felt too agitated to sit down myself. I walked up and down restlessly, doubtless betraying the level of my inner nervousness to anyone who might be watching. Fortunately, there were few passengers waiting for the York train.

I did not relax until, having changed

platforms at York, waited an interminable forty minutes and caught the train for Scarborough, I slumped back in a window seat.

As the countryside sped away at the side of me, I felt I was leaving my whole life behind. The realisation came upon me that if it were not for the twins, there was nothing I wanted to return for. If I had allowed myself, I could have become very depressed. But I took a tight hold, reminded myself I was getting away for a few days in order to gain strength to return to that life. I must not let my imagination run free and visualise any other outcome.

I would take this opportunity of a few days and come to terms fully with what had happened, prepare myself mentally for the reality of my future life.

A picture crossed my mind of the white-faced Mrs Huggett in Nightingale Ward. Had she also felt like this when she was discharged? For her there had been no children to return to.

A feeling of shame came over me. How could I dismiss so lightly the fact I was blessed with three young sons, all of whom still very much needed their mother? I made a solemn bargain with myself. I would be a good mother when I returned, I would put the children's needs before my own. Whatever this coming week held for me, at the end of it, I would return to take up life with Charles and the boys. The children would come first in my scale of priorities, I determined. Having firmly settled that in my mind I mentally freed myself to look forward to the coming days and whatever they might bring.

Leaning forward in my seat, I felt anticipation rise in me as I watched the countryside changing as the train wound its way along the scenic route, heading for Scarborough.

In contrast to the main line impersonal train that had carried me to York, this shabby and battered local train had a cosy, almost homely, feel about it. It seemed to rattle and sway joyfully along the tracks, as eager as its holiday makers to arrive at the seaside. I allowed myself the indulgence of enjoying the ride until quite abruptly, with a clanging and a hissing, the train suddenly ran into Scarborough station and came to a shuddering halt.

I picked up my suitcase and handbag and stepped out onto the platform. I had already decided that the easiest thing to do being a complete stranger here would be to find a taxi and ask for the bus depot where I could catch a bus for Sandsend. I passed over my ticket, hurried through the barrier and emerged into the warm autumn sunshine.

Before I had time to look for a taxi, a figure came striding towards me. My heart flipped over and a trembling sensation of extreme happiness ran right through me.

Milo Kent put out his hand. 'Here, let me take that.'

In a dream, I handed over my suitcase. 'I'd no idea you were meeting me.'

He smiled ruefully. 'An hour ago, neither did I.' Then we were both smiling.

'I find these sudden impulses very hard to understand,' he added, looking at me sideways. 'I think it's possibly on a par with your acceptance to stay here. The old subconscious knew perfectly well what it was going to do but it took the conscious self quite by surprise.'

'That's it exactly,' I nodded. 'I felt just like that when I agreed to come, as though I had known all along that I would.'

'Come on then, I'll show you where Horizon House is.'

We walked across to his black Daimler and he stowed the suitcase in the boot. 'It isn't far,' he said. 'A little farther north and a swing round back onto the coast road again. It's got a beautiful bay. Have you ever been to

Sandsend before?'

I shook my head. 'Never.'

'Very beautiful. It isn't your south coast, not pretty, pretty,' he grinned, 'but the north has a grandeur that goes beyond prettiness. I tell you what, if you'd like, I'll take you to where you can stand and look over the bay from the top of the cliffs before we go to Horizon House. What do you say?'

'I'd really like that.'

'Good as done then.' He spun the wheel expertly and turned out of the station car park, headed north.

The view from the cliffs at Sandsend was all he had promised. It was a glorious autumn day with blue sky and bright sunshine. The tops of the waves as they lifted high before crashing forward in the bay below caught and reflected the glinting light and I watched them roll up the sand in long, stretching, wet fingers.

There were very few people dotted about and the whole scene spread out before me induced a feeling of space and order and overall tranquil timelessness. I stood, feeling the breeze catch my light summer dress and flutter it against my bare legs and already it seemed I was taking the first steps to finding and freeing my real self.

I turned and looked at him. He was

standing watching me with a gentle look on his face.

'Thank you,' I murmured. 'It's perfect, exactly what I need.'

He nodded. 'Most of the ladies who come here to Horizon house say the same thing. That, for me, is my own personal reward and satisfaction.'

For a second or two, a shadow of pain seemed to cross his face but then just as quickly it was gone. I hadn't imagined it. I was left with the impression this man was no stranger himself to personal suffering.

If so, it might be that we could both be instrumental in each other's healing.

★   ★   ★

Horizon House proved to be a large Georgian property set in its own grounds and reached along a tree-lined winding drive. On either side of the wide porch grew Virginia creepers — an absolute picture of red and green foliage — cloaking the facing wall of the building giving it a softened welcoming aspect.

We had taken the coast road round the bay and turned off down a narrow private road from which the entrance gates led off. Milo Kent followed the curve of the gravel drive round to the rear of the house. To one side was a small car park in which stood about a dozen vehicles but he parked up close to the rear entrance and we stepped out.

He lifted my suitcase from the boot and we walked through into the rear hall. Judging by the delicious smell emanating from behind a swing door, it obviously led directly to the kitchen.

A young woman in a blue uniform came down the hall to meet us. Milo Kent set down the suitcase and introduced us.

'Maggie, this is Emma, one of our patients for the coming week.'

'Very good, sir.' She smiled at me and picked up the suitcase. 'Perhaps you would like to follow me. I'll show you your room.' I was about to walk away when he stopped me.

'We don't stand on any ceremony here, it's strictly Christian names only.' He smiled. 'I'm sure you'll find everything satisfactory, and I'll be along later to see how you're settling in. Lunch will be at one o'clock in the dining room.'

'Thank you very much.' I tried to emulate the warm yet formal manner that he had adopted since we'd arrived at Horizon House. There was a hidden undercurrent between us which we both, without saying so, had acknowledged. I knew it must be hidden from the staff.

He, in his capacity as Consultant and owner of Horizon House, had his reputation and position to uphold and I, as a married woman, also needed to retain my good name. Whatever might or might not develop between us this coming week, if it was on a more personal level, it would have to be kept secret to safeguard both of us.

These thoughts went through my mind as I followed Maggie's retreating figure up the wide, carpeted staircase and along the landing at the top. The house was much larger than I had imagined on first sight, proving to have an L-shaped extension that went quite a long way and housed a fair number of private rooms.

'I do hope you're not superstitious.' Maggie turned her head and gave me a quick smile as she set down the suitcase in front of one of the doors. She fished in her uniform pocket and produced the key. 'It's number thirteen . . . ' She waited with eyebrow raised.

'That's fine,' I said, 'I'm not superstitious.'

'Oh good.' She opened the door and showed me in.

It was a delightful room furnished in soft lavender with a crushed strawberry carpet, with matching floral curtains and bedspread tastefully combining the two colours.

The double bed itself had a brass open-work headboard and in front of the matching bedside cabinets lay two white sheepskin rugs. Built-in wardrobes finished in white and picked out with gold ran the full length of one wall and incorporated into them was an arched alcove that formed a dressing table with a velvet-topped stool. There was a small fluorescent light above the inset mirror and reflected in it was a crystal bowl filled with pot-pourri petals from which drifted an exquisite lavender perfume that was both relaxing and sensual.

Maggie walked across the room and opened a door that I had mistakenly thought was a full-length mirror. 'This is your personal bathroom.'

The whole room was tiled from floor to ceiling in the most delicate shade of lavender. The bathroom suite was a matching colour with a quilted front to the bath. There was a gleaming chromium ring on the wall from which hung a thick, neatly draped white towel.

On the vanity unit itself was an array of different bath essences and soaps. The deep pile carpet here again, was a crushed strawberry with matching bath mats. The whole impression I gained was one of pampered, serene comfort. Whoever had designed the interior of this place knew exactly how to cocoon, uplift and restore a woman's spirit. Behind it all was the unmistakable hand impeccably providing the right touch of the man himself. The whole of this place emphasised it was Milo Kent's domain.

'I'll leave you to settle in.' Maggie's voice brought me back down to earth from wherever I had been floating. 'If there is anything you are short of, please don't hesitate to say. There's a bell push by the bed. I do hope you'll be comfortable.'

She whisked away closing the bedroom door behind her, leaving me by myself in this beautiful Nirvana. I had not the slightest doubt that this week was going to be the most magical of my whole life.

I walked over to the mirrored alcove and sat down on the strawberry velvet stool and let my hands glide over the polished surface, exploring the contours of the crystal bowl filled with pot-pourri. Everything in this house spoke of love and caring and compassion — down to the smallest detail.

Rising, I went over to the window. Outside white painted wrought ironwork enclosed a small balcony and I opened the French window and stepped outside leaning on the rail and looking out over the gardens and grounds.

Here again, everything was in perfect order and soothingly arranged to draw the eye down the winding pathways, between the flower beds and on through the rose covered arches to a wide sweep of green lawn. In the centre I could see a small lake shaped rather like a figure of eight spanned at the narrowest part by a delicate Japanese style wooden bridge and surrounded by elegant shrubs and willow trees.

I felt a catch in my throat at the tranquil beauty and thanked God that I had accepted the chance to come here to heal, to be restored and made whole again.

I glanced at my watch; it was already nearly one o'clock. Hurriedly now, I lifted my suitcase onto the bed and released the catches, taking out my clothes and placing them on the hangers provided in the fitted wardrobe. I stowed the case away out of sight on the shelf above the rail and went through with my sponge bag to the bathroom.

I washed my hands, combed my hair and repaired the little make-up that I usually wore. Another glance at my watch and, somewhat reluctantly, I left the room, locking the door behind me, and hastened down the wide staircase to lunch.

There was no sign of Milo but I simply mingled with a cluster of women who had gathered in the hall and allowed myself to be swept along with them into the dining room.

Inside about half a dozen small tables were laid for lunch with pristine white cloths and shining cutlery. In the centre of each table stood a narrow cut-glass flower vase containing a single white rose. From hidden speakers, Mozart's piano concerto number twenty-one was playing very softly.

I chose a seat nearest to the wide bay window overlooking the gardens. It all seemed like a fabulous dream. A slim young woman took the seat opposite me and smiled nervously.

'Isn't it just . . . ' she began and then gave up and simply spread her hands.

'Oh yes, it is.'

She looked round with open admiration. 'Wouldn't it be wonderful to come here on your honeymoon?'

'With the right man,' I agreed.

At that moment, Milo Kent came into the room.

11

Milo Kent weaved his way between the tables and went to stand at the top end of the dining room. As if on cue, Mozart's twenty-first came to an end and all of us turned expectantly to listen to what he was going to say.

'Good afternoon, ladies. I thought I'd have a word before you begin lunch and then I won't need to interrupt you any further today. Would everyone here last week please bear with me whilst I bring the new ladies up to date with the information they need to know.' He paused, looking round and smiling.

'As well as residents, we also have day visitors here and there are numerous facilities available for each and every one of you. I'd like you to feel free to take advantage of any or all of these. They include: heated swimming pool, sauna, facial and/or Swedish massage, spiritual healing, exercises to music in the gym and yoga. For those who like open-air pursuits, there are tennis courts behind the car park and for those who feel a little more adventurous, turn right out of the gates and a few yards down you will see the entrance to Parklands Riding Stables. Horses are provided, ready tacked-up, for hacking out.

'All these services are available and covered by the cost of your fee.

'If anyone wishes to speak to me or see me on matters concerning their health, my office is on the first floor, room seven. If I am already engaged, the receptionist will be happy to book you in for a specific appointment.

'I wish each and every one of you, when you leave here, to feel that you have gained not only in bodily health but on all levels of your personal wellbeing.

'Thank you all very much.'

Following his words, there was a spasmodic clapping but he quickly held up a silencing hand. 'Do enjoy your meal.'

The slim young woman opposite to me, I later learned was called Lucy, leaned forward and whispered, 'He's so caring. He seems to set just the right tone.'

I nodded and reached for my spoon as the waitress set down a bowl of hot celery soup in front of me. Somehow, I didn't trust myself to answer her. I didn't want to let any feelings I had show, either through the quality of vibration in my words or in my expression. But every time I saw Milo, my feelings toward him increased in depth.

Following the soup, we were offered a choice of smoked ham or salmon with side salad and steaming hot baby new potatoes. Even before I could indicate my preference for fish, being a vegetarian, the waitress had served me with salmon. Following the salad there was fresh fruit and a choice of beverages.

'Did you have celery soup to start?' I enquired of Lucy.

'Oh no,' she said, looking rather puzzled, 'mine was chicken.'

I simply nodded and continued with my lunch.

Milo knew from my hospital notes that I was a vegetarian, although, naughtily, I did eat fish. Unobtrusively, he had provided food that he knew I would like and had instructed the waitresses accordingly. How considerate the man was. My respect for him increased enormously.

Before the meal was over, Lucy and I were chatting easily. I learned that she had been here once before, nearly a year ago when she had lost her first baby. Now the poor woman had just suffered a stillborn birth. My heart went out to her. She reminded me so much of Mrs Huggett in Nightingale Ward.

I told her about the baby I had recently lost

and her sympathy for me was genuine and touching.

'It helped so very much last year when I came here to Horizon House,' she said. 'I couldn't seem to get over losing my baby at all, and yet after a week when I went home again, it was like Mr Kent said it would be. The healing is not just on a physical level. Somehow, it seems to uplift your spirit too, makes you feel able to cope when you get home.'

'I certainly hope so,' I said. 'It seems such a wilful extravagance, the cost of staying here, being totally selfish for a whole week.'

'I disagree,' she said earnestly. 'What is the cost compared to feeling you are able to start life again, able to do your best for your husband, everyone? I know last time I went home, I just couldn't wait to see my dear Michael again. It was as though we had just got married, I suppose. It made me feel so loving towards him — feeling well.' Her eyes looked far away as she said it and I waited, knowing she wanted to say more.

'It was almost straight away,' she continued in a very low voice, 'that I managed to conceive and, of course, that completed the happiness.'

Tears filled her blue eyes and overflowed down her cheeks. Instinctively, I put my hand out and squeezed hers.

'It's early days yet, Lucy, give yourself time. Remember how you felt last time when you left Horizon House to go back home. You'll feel like that again.'

She sniffed and dabbed her face with a hankie. 'Yes, yes, you're right.' She stood up and pushed back her chair. 'I may see you at dinner this evening. I think I shall go for a rest now.'

I, too, left the dining room but didn't feel in the least like going to lie down. Through the broad bay window the gardens looked so inviting, bathed in golden autumn sunshine and I felt it a sheer crime to waste the chance of walking through them. It was possible this Indian summer would come to a close at any time.

I wandered out through the glass doors and into the flower gardens. Following the twists and turns of the pathways as they wound their way between lawns and flower beds, I came to the arch over which a pink rambling rose sprawled in abandoned profusion, filling the air with a beautiful perfume. It was as if it had been grown especially for its perfume and not for visual beauty. I had not realised before how much scent influenced one's mood.

The perfume wasn't simply delightful to

smell, it also had a most beautifully soothing effect and my wandering steps slowed down even more as I went through the arch and out onto the wide, sweeping lawn and along the bank of the lake.

Heady with the exhilaration of personal freedom, I crossed the narrow wooden bridge over the lake and took a path between the willow trees that led towards a wood. It was larger than I had thought and, not wishing to get lost, I kept to the main path. I was so completely enthralled by my surroundings that I almost bumped into someone at the junction of the main pathway and a narrow side path where there was a small notice that read 'Private'.

'Hello, Emma.' The familiar voice pulled me up short. It was Milo. 'Everything all right?'

'Absolutely fine.'

'Good. I like the ladies who come here to feel completely at ease.' Whilst he was talking, his eyes held mine and there was no denying the positive vibrations linking us. They were so strong they seemed almost tangible. 'Would you object to my walking with you?'

'Not at all. In fact, I'd very much like you to.'

I was about to continue on down the main path when he shook his head slightly. 'Would you allow me? There's something I'd like to show you.'

I obediently turned and fell into step beside him. He retraced his steps back past the 'Private' notice and down the side path. We were almost out of the wood itself and heading downhill when he paused and pointed. 'There, do you see?'

Just a short way ahead of us, in a dip half hidden by trees, stood a small log cabin. 'That's where I stay — when I'm here,' he said simply. 'I call it my retreat.'

I caught my breath. 'It's like something out of a fairy tale.'

'Well, you see, when I bought Horizon House and the land, I knew I wouldn't wish to stay in the house itself. Apart from tying up the valuable accommodation, I needed somewhere to get away from the pressure and just be myself, relax. So when the builders were converting the house to how I wanted it, I had them build this small cabin.' He looked sideways at me. 'I don't normally show anyone. I had a small notice placed at the junction of the paths, but there aren't many who wander further than the edge of the wood in any case.'

I turned and looked at him. 'But you've shown me. You brought me here on purpose to show me.'

'Yes, I have, haven't I?' A smile flitted across his face. 'I wanted to, Emma.' His voice was very soft. 'When I am in your presence, I act only on instinct. Do you find that very odd, reprehensible? Taking into account my position?'

I looked into those warm hazel eyes that were serious now as he seemed almost to question himself for motive. I laid a hand on his arm.

'No. I don't think it's the slightest bit reprehensible. If you were to ask me what I really think . . . ' I hesitated, searching for the right words to express myself honestly. 'I feel as though we have known each other for millions of years. This instinctive feeling you say you have, would it surprise you to know that I also feel exactly the same? That I feel it is almost an unfurling of destiny that we have met?'

It was Milo's turn now to seize both my hands. 'Emma, I hardly dared to say this, for all I feel it so very strongly. There is a knowing in the core of my being, at soul level, that tells me you and I are special.' He hurried on, 'I don't mean in an egotistical way, I mean, special to each other — in a way that I have never, ever felt with another human being before.'

How long we stood there holding hands, I

have really no idea. Time was not a factor. It didn't enter into it. The whole universe seemed suspended in time and there were just the two of us standing on that wooded hillside in the sunshine. We gazed so deeply into each other's eyes that it was like going down into the depths of a lagoon.

All the striving and searching I had ever done in my life totally ceased. I had never before known such complete contentment and peace, and I simply stood and gazed at him. I felt truly alive and blissfully happy for the first time in my life.

There was no need to ask Milo if he were feeling the same. This complete harmony could only be experienced by two souls inextricably intertwined.

A church clock, far below in the valley, chimed the hour and slowly we became aware of our surroundings again.

★ ★ ★

For the next three days, the only time I saw Milo was at mealtimes.

Life fell into a pattern at Horizon House and each day, in addition to the normal range of facilities, we had something special on the agenda of activities.

Milo always came into the dining room just

165

before breakfast and informed us of the day's programme but apart from that, he and I had had no further contact. Part of me, the strictly brought up, straight-laced side of me, rejoiced. 'For your own good, my girl,' it said — and made me feel very depressed.

But the free spirit within me, my true self, cried out with longing to be close to him. So wrong — so right, which one should it be? Depressed and downhearted without him close to me? Or, when I was in his presence, to be filled with joy and uplifted on all the levels within me, from the physical, emotional and mental to the highest spiritual?

I lay awake in bed at night and thought exclusively of him and was filled with a great happiness. Always, the following day, when I only saw him so briefly before breakfast, I was conscious of a yawning, empty coldness. I had to fight down the urge to leave my seat and run after him as he left the dining room. This was no adolescent attachment — it penetrated to greater depths than that. Depths that decreed he and I were like the two halves of a broken eggshell, useless by themselves but, put together, they formed a perfect whole.

During the day, to fill that yearning emptiness within me, I sampled various goodies that were on offer and experienced for the first time the remarkable and releasing properties of massage, spiritual healing and reflexology.

I had not thought to take a swimming costume with me although I could swim, but costumes were available in a variety of sizes. Again, my respect for Milo increased. He seemed to have thought of everything.

Every day immediately before lunch, I made a point of going for a swim in the warm pool. Most of the time, I took part as one of a group and yet at the same time an individual on my own.

There seemed to be points during the day when the other convalescent women welcomed a chat about what had brought them here but whilst participating in the different activities within Horizon House, chatting didn't enter into it. Perhaps this was the reason the therapies were so successful. The whole self was given to the particular form of therapy being undergone and, by its very nature, was an individualistic experience.

However, mealtimes were one of those earmarked slots in the day given over not simply to the necessary business of eating but the chance it afforded for close association with others.

I always sat at the same table in the same chair and was pleased to discover that Lucy did the same. During the short time we spent in each other's company, we had become not only acquaintances but friends. However, although I enjoyed both the food and the company, I desperately longed to be with Milo.

On the morning of the fourth day, I felt I could stand our enforced separation no longer. It would have been easier had I not seen him for those few brief minutes each morning.

But on the fourth morning when I came out of the bathroom, I noticed a small, white folded piece of paper lying just inside the bedroom door. It had obviously been slid underneath as the door was still locked. Intrigued, I sat down on the dressing table stool and unfolded it. My heart leapt wildly. It was from Milo.

'If you wish to see the inside of the retreat, remove the penny I have left beneath your napkin at the breakfast table, and place it outside your bedroom door. If you prefer not to, believe me, I *do* understand.'

There they were again — those three words.

Instantly, I was back in Nightingale Ward, lying in that narrow bed between the stiff, white sheets feeling I had been broken into little pieces. And seated by the side of the bed, looking down at me with that immeasurable warmth showing in his eyes, was Milo. He had repeated those words — just as surely as if he had stood beside me and uttered them.

The real question wasn't could I resist seeing the inside of the log cabin, but rather, could I resist seeing Milo?

This linking current, however, was so powerful a force, neither of us had any choice.

We were both helpless to resist.

12

I took the note through to the bathroom and hid it in my sponge bag. Then went and stood in front of the open wardrobe and deliberated which of my clothes was the most becoming. Finally, I chose a blue, full-skirted summer dress and tried a twirl in front of the mirror. The dress flared out from my body before falling gently back into place, emphasising my slim hips. It not only made me look good, it made me feel good, too.

I felt a strange mixture of self-assurance and nervousness as I locked the bedroom door behind me. As I began to descend the staircase, I was actually trembling.

Entering the dining room, I walked swiftly over to my table by the window and put my hand on the napkin, drawing it towards me as I sat down. Without looking down, I felt a small, flat weight drop onto my thigh. The napkin lay innocently on top of the thin material of my dress but underneath, the penny seemed to be burning its way through to my skin. I undid the clasp on my handbag and with the napkin acting as concealment, my fingers closed over the penny and I dropped it unseen into my handbag.

I felt the guilty, red flush rising in my cheeks and without raising my head, cast a quick glance across the room. There were only one or two already seated and nobody had noticed me.

I took a deep, shuddering breath and poured a glass of iced fruit juice . . .

* * *

When the rest of the women had gathered for breakfast, Milo came in and informed us that today's special activity was to be horse riding along the beach at three-thirty. Jodhpurs and riding hats were available at the stable office.

A buzz of interest ran around the room following his words. He smiled, wished us all good day and left the dining room. Not once did he look directly at me.

'Oooh, that sounds nice, doesn't it?' Lucy helped herself to milk on her cereal. 'I think I'll go for a ride. What about you, Emma?'

'I may,' I said, realising I was being noncommittal but my thoughts were else-where. I had no idea what time of day Milo had in mind for granting me the privilege of showing me his personal domain. 'I'll think about it,' I added, seeing the rather quizzical look Lucy gave me.

171

'I don't think you have to be an expert rider,' she went on reassuringly. 'I'm sure it will only be walking and, possibly, trotting along the beach — and it's a perfect day.'

She glanced up at the window, the sun was streaming through and for autumn it was amazing, a true Indian summer. I didn't answer, although I felt mean.

'Well, I shall go.' She lifted her chin a little and said determinedly, 'I've come here to begin life again. And today seems a pretty good day to start living.' Her words struck a responsive chord within me.

'I couldn't agree with you more,' I burst out impulsively, pushing back my chair and standing up. Suddenly, I couldn't wait to get upstairs to my room and place the penny outside my bedroom door.

But once I'd done it, I paced nervously up and down inside my bedroom. I had absolutely no idea when Milo intended to check whether the penny was there or not.

Finally, I took a grip on myself, opened the doors onto the balcony and went outside. There was a white painted, wrought-iron seat and I sat down and looked out over the gardens taking in deep breaths of the soft, scented air, trying to calm myself.

I had sat for perhaps half an hour but the suspense was still building up inside. Taking one last deep breath, I rose and went back into the bedroom intent upon checking whether the penny had disappeared or not when I noticed a piece of paper had been slid under the door — for the second time that morning. I snatched up the paper and read it.

'Thank you for your trust and if you're agreeable, I'd like to take you out riding on the beach immediately after lunch at two o'clock,' it began. 'This will allow an hour's ride and ensure that we're back at the stables before the other ladies from Horizon House arrive for their ride at three-thirty. Following our ride, I suggest we take a roundabout walk and come through the back entrance of the woods and call in at the retreat. Obviously, I'd prefer it if you don't mention this to anyone. I'll meet you at the gates of Parkland Stables at two o'clock.' It was signed Milo.

I saw the reasoning behind why he had set a time for the other women to take their beach ride. Judging by the murmur that had gone around the dining room, quite a few of them did intend to go for a ride. That meant that Milo and I would be undisturbed.

I felt a guilty thrill run through me. But even as I shivered deliciously with anticipation, I chided myself. Milo must take precautions against being seen to indulge in unseemly conduct with one of his patients. And going alone with me to the retreat would obviously be construed as that. I was only too aware the whole of his career could be blighted beyond recognition. He could be struck off the register and lose his livelihood, which in turn, meant all the hundreds of women who would have undoubtedly benefitted from his skill and loving care would lose out.

Although I didn't diminish the need to maintain my own cloak of respectability, it was very clear that it was Milo towards whom I felt protective in maintaining a shield of secrecy.

I went into lunch at one o'clock as usual. Lucy had beaten me to it and I hurried over and slid into my seat opposite her. 'I don't think I'll have a great deal for lunch today,' I said. My stomach was turning over and over with nervous excitement. 'I think I'll just opt for soup and a roll.'

She nodded. 'Actually, I was thinking along those lines myself. Bouncing up and down on a horse's back this afternoon might not be a good idea on a full stomach.' We both smiled. 'Have you decided yet, if you are going to have a ride?'

I felt the heat rising in my cheeks. 'I haven't decided quite what I *am* doing this afternoon,' I said. Well, at least that was the truth. 'I do intend to spend quite a while outside with the weather being so good. I simply adore wandering through the gardens.'

To my relief, she let the subject drop and instead began to tell me eagerly about the benefits she felt she had gained from that morning's session of reflexology. I was quite happy to let her prattle on without interrupting and busied myself with breaking the fresh crispy bread roll and spooning up the delicious soup.

Probably because I had let Lucy do most of the talking, I finished my simple meal first. 'If you'll excuse me, Lucy, I think I'll go up and have a few minutes lie down on my bed before I decide what I'm going to do this afternoon.'

She paused with the spoon hallway to her lips. 'Good idea. If I don't see you before, I shall probably see you tonight at dinner.' I nodded and made my escape.

I hurried to my room and changed my high heels for some flat shoes. Milo had said that riding clothes were available at the stables but obviously suitable shoes were needed. Not only that, I thought guiltily, afterwards we were going to walk by a circuitous route through the countryside before reaching the retreat. I remembered his previous thoughtfulness regarding my diet and my respect for him grew.

At ten minutes to two, I shakily applied fresh lipstick and sprayed on some L'Aimant perfume before descending the wide staircase. As unobtrusively as possible, I left Horizon House and went out of the gates turning right. It was only a few yards up the road to Parklands Stables and sure enough as I turned in at the gates, I could see Milo's black Daimler in the car park. I walked quickly up the gravel drive, my heart beating furiously.

As I drew level with the car, Milo stepped out, locking the door. We stood for a moment or two staring at each other, communicating silently. Behind his confident assured manner I could detect a nervousness.

'I'm ready, whenever you are,' I said.

A smile lit up his face and the nervousness dropped away from him. 'Come on, then,' he said.

And I felt like a child again, playing truant from school.

We walked round to the rear of the building into the stable yard itself. It was built in an 'L' shape and the stables all had half-open doors from which horses' heads appeared at the sound of our footsteps. The unmistakable smell of warm horse filled my nostrils and took me back several years to when Adam had been keen to learn to ride. Charles and I had taken him to the small local riding school and I had learned to ride at the same time.

Milo led the way past the short arm of the 'L' to a door at the corner which had the word office written across it in bold black letters. He knocked.

'Feel free,' called a woman's cultured voice and we went in.

'Hello, Mrs Protheroe.' Milo thrust out his right hand. 'How are you?'

'Very well, thanks.'

'Do you think I could have two horses, please? My usual and, shall we say, possibly one like Sadie, for my friend, Mrs Wetherford?' He introduced us. We both nodded.

'I believe Ross is free and so is Sadie. I'll have Marion tack them up for you immediately.

'Ross is my usual horse,' explained Milo.

'Have you done much riding, Mrs Wetherford?' Mrs Protheroe enquired delicately.

'Truthfully, I think you could say I'm simply a beginner,' I admitted.

'I'm a great believer in honesty, myself,' she smiled. 'I think Sadie would be just right for you. Do go ahead and kit yourself out.' She rose and indicated a side door in the office before going outside in search of Marion.

I went through to the changing room and put on cream jodhpurs and a short sleeved shirt, and found a navy velvet hard hat that fitted perfectly.

On my return to the office, Milo said, 'I didn't want you to miss out on this afternoon's ride. It's a bit unfair if all the others could take advantage and you couldn't. So, I thought you and I could go on our own.'

'That was very thoughtful of you, but then, I'm beginning to realise what a caring, thoughtful man you are. It sounds a dream ride.'

'It is. It's always a great favourite with the ladies from Horizon House.'

The sound of hooves clattering over concrete outside drew us both out of the door. Ross was a big, seventeen hands black gelding, whereas Sadie was little more than a pony at fourteen two, a very pale bay with a pretty, delicately formed head and kind eye. I fell for her immediately. Marion passed Ross's reins to Milo and left him to it.

'Would you like to go over to the mounting block?' she asked.

'I think I'll be OK. Sadie's not very big.' Marion held the mare's head and I gathered up the reins in my left hand, angled the stirrup and put my left foot in, giving a spring off my right leg and swinging across the saddle. 'It's a bit like riding a bike,' I joked to Marion as I checked the length of the leathers and put my feet into the irons.

She nodded. 'Have a lovely ride.'

'Thanks, I'm sure we will.'

'All right?' Milo shouted over his shoulder as he circled Ross round.

'Fine,' I called back, 'lead on.' And I squeezed Sadie's round sides and clicked to her.

We walked sedately down the zig-zag track that sloped downwards and eventually reached the beach. Staid as undoubtedly Sadie was, when her hooves felt the sand beneath them, she skittered and tossed her head making the bridle jingle. Her nostrils flared, taking in the strong whiff of salt air and her ears pricked forwards in anticipation.

'Shorten your reins,' Milo instructed. 'Let's try a trot, eh?'

Side by side, we trotted steadily along the very edge of the breakers as they creamed in long, reaching fingers up the firm sand. Above us, elegant, white seagulls dipped and soared on the air currents, mewling plaintively, their cries carrying in the stiff breeze blowing in off the sea. Ross's tail spayed out raggedly as the wind caught it and Sadie's ears flicked back and forth as I murmured soft encouraging noises to her.

There was no-one else on the beach at all and in no time I had found my 'seat' and could rise to the trot effortlessly again. Milo reined Ross back and we walked along contentedly, the only sound the swish of the breakers coming in and the muffled clop of the hooves. Milo smiled across at me as our horses drew closer and our legs brushed.

'A good idea?' he asked.

'A very good idea.'

But once our eyes had met from so short a distance it was very hard to break free. We both realised at the same moment that we had let the reins fall limp against the saddle pommels and were no longer in charge of the horses. Once again, we were experiencing that unique intermingling sensation.

'I think,' Milo said thickly, 'we had better shake this pair up and trot on, don't you? They'll be thinking we've gone to sleep in the saddle.'

'Hmmm,' I murmured, reluctant to burst the magic bubble that surrounded us, 'I suppose if we don't we shall have all the other ladies riding down the sands and overtaking us.'

He laughed out loud. 'Come on, then.' He

kicked Ross on and the big horse responded. 'Would you feel comfortable with a canter?' he called over his shoulder as the big horse put space between himself and Sadie.

'I think so, I'm more confident now I've done a trot.'

'Kick on, then.'

Obediently, I kicked and Sadie responded. We cantered down the empty beach with the wind whistling past our faces, lifting the horses' manes and tails whilst the golden sands flashed by beneath the hooves. It was blissfully exhilarating.

We had cantered for almost half a mile when Milo lifted a hand and signalled for me to take a pull.

'You look marvellous,' he complimented, whirling Ross around so the horses were facing one another. 'Coming here is doing you the world of good. You've a healthy pink in your cheeks and your eyes look alive and dancing.'

'I really enjoyed that,' I said, panting, 'it was thrilling. I haven't had a canter on a horse for several years.'

'Perhaps you ought to continue when you get home, it obviously agrees with you.'

'Being here, with you, agrees with me,' I said. I turned Sadie and started to trot back along the beach.

He flicked the reins and urged his horse upsides. Companionably, the horses walked side by side back towards the stables.

'I wanted to be alone with you very much, Emma. Ever since you came I've had this need just to be in your presence. I've been fighting down this urge until it's become unbearable.'

'I know, it's exactly the same for me. It was torture to see you just for those few short minutes in the morning, in the dining room.'

'I've spent most of the last three nights lying awake,' Milo continued. 'I see your face all the time and particularly, your beautiful blue eyes. When I look at you, I feel I go down into them and drown. It's a wonderful sensation.'

I bent my head and looked at the bay's withers moving so smoothly and rhythmically in front of me as Sadie shortened the distance back to her stable.

'I can't begin to describe what your eyes do to me,' I whispered. 'The warmth in them melts every cell in my body. I feel . . . I feel . . . I'm drawn in through your eyes to the whole of your body, we both melt down, intermingle — we become one.' I knew the blush on my cheeks then was not the healthy, pink one but the guilty red.

For long moments the silence stretched between us and he didn't reply. I glanced swiftly across at him, my cheeks burning more furiously than ever. But the tender look on his face reassured me.

'That must have taken a great deal of courage. I'm so honoured you feel able to tell me.' He swallowed hard. 'We're so in tune, it's beyond wonderful.'

I felt a surge of joy and also relief as though a tight spring had been released inside me and the tension that I had not known I had been holding onto drained away and I was filled not only to the brim but overflowing with sweet happiness.

Milo shifted both reins to his left hand and reached out for me. I took his hand in mine. The horses seemed quite content to jog along side by side and Milo and I didn't need to say anything. We were as completely in harmony as it was possible to get.

When we reached the zig-zag track leading back up and away from the beach, we reluctantly released hands. I felt as though I was a pin in the grip of a powerful magnet, so strong was my desire to maintain physical contact with him. It was fortunate that the track was a little difficult to negotiate and required concentration. I had of necessity to hold both reins at one particular steep part, to stand up in the stirrups and lean forward taking my weight off the saddle and Sadie's back to help her on the incline.

Back at the stables, we handed over both horses to Marion's care. I rubbed Sadie's velvet nose, and palmed her one of the lumps of sugar that I had taken from the breakfast table that morning. I slipped a second one to Milo. Laughing, he pulled Ross's ear affectionately, and gave it to him. Both horses crunched in delight at this unexpected treat.

I went into the changing room at the back of the stable office and hastily swapped from jodhpurs to my blue summer dress, restoring my gold hoop earrings that I had removed before donning the riding hat. I handed the clothing back to Mrs Protheroe.

'Thank you so much. I really enjoyed that ride, it was the first one I've had for a long time, but I think it's reactivated the bug in me.'

She smiled. 'Come back, any time. We'll be very pleased to see you.'

Milo shook her hand. 'Charge it to my account, as usual.'

We walked out and round to his car. Milo cast a quick glance at his watch and gave a sharp exclamation. 'If we don't hurry, we're going to run slap into the other ladies coming for their three-thirty rides.'

I had no idea time had flown so quickly. 'We can't risk meeting them. What are we going to do?'

'I think it might be better, Emma, if you were to walk back on your own. Come through the gardens at Horizon House and I'll meet you at the junction of the paths in the wood. There isn't time to walk the long way round which I'd planned.'

'Fine by me. We must keep it secret.' I grimaced. 'That makes it sound so sordid — but nothing could be further from the truth.'

We parted and I walked back along the lane. The black Daimler swept past as I walked towards the entrance of the convalescent home. I blessed Milo's forethought as shortly afterwards a straggling group of women wended their way out of the main doors as I arrived.

It would never have done to be seen coming back in Milo's car. Even if questions had not been asked, there may have been raised eyebrows. I desperately wanted to retain Milo's unblemished reputation. There was no way I would wish to compromise him.

★ ★ ★

I walked through the wood and found him waiting for me at the junction of the paths beside the notice that read 'Private'. He stepped forward, took my elbow gently and guided me through the trees towards the retreat.

13

We said little as we walked along the woodland path but simply being in his presence elevated my consciousness. I was acutely aware of the birdsong that filled the woods and the warm pressure of his fingers against my bare skin.

We came to the break in the trees and before us, set in its own peaceful dip, was the log cabin.

'I appreciate you bringing me here, Milo,' I murmured. 'Have you ever brought anyone else?'

'Never,' he said, without looking at me.

I felt humble, as though he had allowed me a glimpse into the private recesses of his mind.

Reaching the heavy, wooden door, he unlocked it, gave it a push and stood back to allow me in. I stepped over the log that formed the doorstep and went inside. The cabin was very simply furnished. The bare boards were stained and polished with a shaggy, cream rug laid before the open fireplace. In the hearth stood a tall, amber vase that held feathery dried grasses, teasels and dark, bitter-chocolate velvet bulrushes. Angled by the side of the hearth was a three-seater settee upholstered in gold.

The two windows which looked out down towards the valley were without curtains but on both window sills stood a brass oil lamp. I nodded towards them. 'Do you use those for lighting?'

'Yes.'

'And do you light fires in the winter?'

'Yes.'

'No electricity?' I queried.

He smiled. 'Actually, I have electricity. Yes, I cheat. But I prefer to keep it all as simple as possible. I find simplicity is good for the soul.'

I looked around and could appreciate his words. He had no television. The only concession to modern living here was a record player.

'Come.' He took my hand. 'Let me show you round. There's not a lot to see.' He tugged me gently and I followed him. At the other end of the living room hung a thick velvet curtain. He drew it aside to reveal the most basic of kitchens. A tiny fridge, an oven with two top rings and a single drainer sink. At shoulder level were narrow wooden cupboards. There was just room to walk in, take two steps each to left and right and walk out again.

'So there you are, that's that,' he said and pulled the curtain back again.

Walking across the living room, he opened a door at the back of the cabin and, once again, stood back as I went before him into his bedroom.

It was small with one window. The pine double bed, draped with an oatmeal, jacquard woven bedspread, had matching bedside cabinets. An oil lamp stood on one and on the other a radio, alarm clock and telephone. A thick rug lay snuggled beside the bed on top of polished boards. The room said far more about the man than he could possibly have guessed. Simple, comfortable, basic requirements necessary for relaxation from the pressures of work, but the means to be recalled to that work and the outside world at a minute's notice.

Milo had stepped across to a curtain fronting an alcove. He drew it back revealing a white, full-sized bath together with shower, handbasin and toilet.

'Nothing like a soak in a warm bath to untie the knots.' He spread his arms wide. 'Well, Mrs Wetherford, now you've seen all the retreat.'

'Please,' I said quickly, 'please, don't call me that name. I want you to call me Emma.'

He inclined his head in agreement.

'Emma.' Once again our eyes met and held but he swiftly broke the connection. 'Come along,' he took my arm, 'we'll go to the living room, have a sit down and a drink. I haven't a lot but I can rustle up mugs of tea or coffee — I think there may even be a bottle of wine.'

I laughed. 'Tea would be lovely.'

He pushed me gently down on the living room settee. 'Sit,' he said firmly.

I grinned. 'Which breed of dog am I, then?'

'You will do as you're told, ma'am, and be waited on.'

A couple of minutes later he reappeared holding two white china beakers. I took one from him gratefully. 'Just what I need.' I sat and sipped contentedly and looked out of the window at the beautiful wooded slopes, all the differing shades of green. He stood watching me over the rim of his mug as he took a drink. 'You look as though you've always lived here. You fit in, perfectly. You belong.'

Now it was my turn to incline my head. 'That's exactly how I feel.' I hadn't realised until that moment just how tensed up I had been over the past few months. It was like taking the plug from a bath filled with water and allowing it to drain effortlessly away.

Milo wandered over and leaned against the open door of the log cabin, looking out, sipping hot tea. 'There's something I must tell you, Emma.'

'Yes?'

'I'm a married man.'

Although I was prepared for him to be married, my heart plummeted and I felt physical pain. 'You already know I'm a married woman,' I said in a low voice.

'Not only that.' Milo turned his head to look at me. 'A married woman with three young sons.'

'Yes.'

'Who you love very much.'

'I love them more than anything else in this world, yes.'

'And your . . . husband? His name is Charles, isn't it?'

'It is. And no, I do not love Charles.'

He nodded, saying nothing.

'Your wife?' I prompted. 'What's her name?'

'Wendy.' The silence stretched.

I tried again. 'Do you have any children?'

'No. Like yourself, we lost an unborn baby.'

'I'm sorry.' His words flashed through my mind. 'I *do* understand.' Now I knew why. 'Do you want to tell me any more?' I asked gently.

'I don't want to — because it's so very painful.' He fixed his gaze far away over the

191

tops of the trees to the distant horizon. Then he went on in a low voice, 'I don't want to, but I *need* to.'

'Then, please . . . '

Hesitantly at first, Milo told me about Wendy. He described her as she had been when they first met: a laughing, carefree, blonde goddess of a girl, vitally alive. Told me of his feelings on their wedding day when he thought he was king of the whole world and could never, ever be any happier. Shared with me tiny details of their life together — until the day of the accident.

I watched his knuckles tighten around the china beaker, turn white, as he went through each and every cruel detail. I found myself catching my breath and was unconscious of the fact that my own fingernails were digging hard into the palms of my hands. I forced myself to remain silent, withholding any platitudes of sorrow that might stop the flow of this torrent of grief and hurt that was gushing out of him after festering inside for eight long years.

Finally, the cleansing was over and Milo came to sit beside me on the settee. I could feel the trembling in his body although we weren't touching. I waited for several minutes whilst he regained his self-control.

'Now it's my turn,' I said, looking at him

face-to-face. 'Believe me, I *do* understand. I also understand why you've chosen this work. I won't degrade it by calling it a career, it's so much more, a lifetime's work. I can appreciate now how you understand what women want, especially women who have suffered a great loss. This is why you excel of course.' I leaned forward and held his hand tightly between both of my own. 'Milo, you don't have to make amends. It wasn't your fault. You mustn't go on blaming yourself, feeling guilty. But you do have to go on with this work. It's vitally important.'

'Thank you, I know the work drives me but I also know I need it — as much as it needs me.'

To give him some space, I picked up the two empty mugs, went through into the miniscule kitchen and made some fresh tea.

I pushed a steaming mug into his hand. 'The catharsis is over. Let's drink to your future now.'

He drew in a shuddering deep breath. 'And, God, how good it feels — to release all of that.'

We sat and sipped in silence. The very atmosphere in the log cabin felt light and free as though we had both released a pressure within us which had been building up, retained for years.

'Do you mind if I choose some music?' I set down the mug and went over and selected a record and put it on at low volume. I came back and curled up on the settee beside him once more.

The player came to life and the beautiful Strauss melody poured into the room.

'How did you know?' Milo looked at me and raised a quizzical eyebrow. 'The 'Blue Danube' is one of my favourites.'

'Intuition?'

We laughed. On a rebound from tension, our spirits danced up high.

Milo rose, setting down his mug of tea. 'You can't play the 'Blue Danube' without waltzing.' He drew me gently into the circle of his arm.

Close together, we circled gracefully within the confines of the log cabin and I couldn't feel the bare boards beneath my feet, I was floating above the ground. I was aware only of the warmth of his body through his shirt and the strength of his arm where it held my waist. He drew me even closer and I buried my face in the hollow of his shoulder, smelt the warm, male scent of him. It was like the freshness of winds blowing over wild moors, salt spray from tides, newly-planed wood, and the warmth of amber as distinctive as Milo himself, tender yet powerful.

I slid my hands around his neck and let my fingertips bury themselves in the blonde, curly hair above his collar. I gave myself up completely to swaying to the seductive, liquid music. This wasn't simply dancing to a beautiful melody, this was dancing to the music of life.

I could hear Milo's voice whispering my name over and over again as his lips brushed my ear and kissed my hair: 'Emma, my Emma, my Emma . . . ' He bent his head, searching for my lips with his own. I tilted my head back and felt him brush across my lips, light as gossamer, covering my cheeks, throat, closed eyelids, with the tiniest, most tender of kisses.

Each and every fibre of my being responded to the tender love for which I had searched — not knowing I'd searched — all my life.

An image came into my mind of the two of us dancing in freedom at the very dawn of time. No log cabin enclosing us now, but a wood, with the early sunlight glistening golden through the rising mist, highlighting the bluebells under the trees, the spring-green leaves on firm, brown branches. Brown like Milo's arms, strong, tanned — yet still vulnerable to love.

Then he was sweeping me up and holding

me close to his muscular chest and I was aware now of the log cabin about us, could feel the warmth of him soaking through my dress, warming my own skin.

And the music rose and fell, glided and swirled and Milo waltzed gracefully with me still in his arms, still covering my face with tiny kisses, through the doorway into the bedroom.

The music followed us, seductive, enticing, beguiling, carrying us along with it in waves of sweet happiness. Carefully, so carefully, he laid me down on the bed. One by one, starting at the neck, he gently undid the row of buttons down the front of my dress and let the thin material fall open. He shed his own clothes and with a swift movement, eased off my remaining clothes.

The music played on and on in my mind and I felt suspended in mid-air. I seemed to hear a female voice whispering, 'It's the music . . . making contact . . . '

And then I was aware only of the firmness of the bed beneath me and the hard warmth of Milo's body above me. His hands spread and stroked and smoothed my whole body, using the very tips of his fingers delicately tracing patterns of exquisite delight on my responsive skin. Brushing the softness of my throat with his lips, Milo lowered his head, burying his face between my breasts, whilst his hands continued to caress and tease and excite me. I'd never experienced this form of love-making ever before. And every cell in my body cried out in delight, embracing the pure outpouring of true love. I had been denied love for so long during my marriage to Charles, it was a revelation to find a man who could want me so much.

His lips sought my nipples, nibbling, kissing, engulfing and lighting fire in me that ran in frissons down my body. His fingertips seemed to track those fires, down, down, down over the small swell of my belly and lower still until they buried themselves in the golden hairs that covered the very essence of my womanhood. And as his fingertips reached their goal, involuntarily, my back arched and I heard myself giving tiny animal cries of ecstasy as they teased and stroked, left and returned, again and again.

Then his hands slid down the inside of my soft inner thighs, kneading, caressing, deliciously tormenting, making me grip his shoulders tightly, lifting myself to him in abandon. My hands slid down the hollow of his back between the shoulder-blades and down past his waist to the rise of his naked buttocks, pressing them close as he thrust himself hard and urgently into me.

And as the sea rushes in to the shore to recede reluctantly before it rushes in again hungrily, so it was with us. Milo's body carried us on the tide of love ebbing and flowing with increasing fervour, expressing physical love on through his hard pulsating masculinity. As both our bodies became one unified body, I felt my whole being melt, liquefy and combine with his and it was impossible to be separated one from the other.

And the sea raged on, until finally, we were gloriously shipwrecked and tossed, shuddering and spent, upon a far distant shore. We lay, cocooned in each other's arms, surrounded it seemed, by a magic bubble of rainbow colours, caressed by warm, soft butterscotch and honey. Love was so indescribably sweet a force, it could not be explained nor described but only experienced and once experienced, could never be forgotten.

Lost in love, we slept and woke and loved again until outside it grew dark and beyond the tiny bedroom window, the stars pricked the sky with brilliant silver light.

Then, and only then, did Milo stir, take his arms from around my body and slide from the bed. 'My darling,' his voice was husky and he reached out with both his hands to me, 'we have to dress, go back; it must be very late. They'll be missing us at Horizon House.'

'No, no.' I tugged his hands. 'I don't want to go back. I don't want to leave you, Milo, I need you.'

'And God, I need you.' He crushed me to him, burying his fingers in my long hair and pulling my head back gently kissing my throat, ears and lips again and again. I felt his body rise and harden against my bare thigh. And still we kissed and caressed. The emptiness of the years and years of waiting was a hunger that could never be satisfied during this lifetime. If we were to make love from now until we died I could never be filled, would always want more of him.

'Are we mad, Milo?' I cried. 'What is happening to us?'

'We're fulfilling our destiny, my darling. Our coming together was written in stone and nothing we could have done would have altered it — or will alter it. It's as inevitable as the earth turning.'

'But it can't last, Milo.'

'I know,' he said, his voice so low I could barely catch the words. 'But it can last for the rest of this week. We'll blank out thoughts of the future, Emma.'

He cupped my face in his hands and stared into my eyes. 'Now is all we have and we must take it. We cannot deny it.'

He released me and reached over, flicking the curtains across the window, blotting out the stars. Then, taking my hand, he led me through into the bathroom and turned on the shower.

We both stood and let the needles of warm water dance and play upon our bodies. There was a dispenser of liquid soap and Milo poured some into my upturned palm, pressed his hand against mine and the liquid oozed and bubbled between our fingers. Gently, we stroked and cleansed one another and allowed the warm water to flow over us. It seemed the two of us were the only beings, not just on earth, but in the whole universe. Coming from water — composed of water — living by water.

We stood entwined within the cascade encircling us — our very own universe — and we wanted nothing more.

PART FIVE

1983

14

The 'Blue Danube' built to a final spiral and the music came to an end. Looking down at her mother with close attention, Thalia said, 'The music, it's making contact . . . You did see that, didn't you?' Excitedly, she twisted round and looked at her three brothers who were also bending over her mother's bed. 'She moved, Adam, she moved!'

'I saw, by God, I saw her move. It has reached her, Thalia.'

'There had to be a reason why she used to love to play the 'Blue Danube',' Thalia said, jumping up. 'Now we know for sure what it was.'

'Yes,' Ian growled, a scowl darkening his face. 'It was the music that she and her lover danced to — before they made love.' His mouth twisted in disgust.

Simon, backing his twin brother as always, gave a curt nod.

'OK, so it's the truth, yes.' Thalia was trembling now. 'But if what Mother has said about her marriage to Father is true — and why should she have lied? — could you not find it in your hearts to have compassion for

203

her in those circumstances?'

None of her three brothers answered.

'Well, you may not, you're at a disadvantage — not being female. But I am and I can see only too clearly Mother's situation. Held in a marriage for the sake of appearances.' She whirled round and pointed a trembling finger at them. 'Don't forget, it was for the sake of you three, when you were children. So before you get on your high and mighty horses, perhaps you'd better think about that. Right now, I'm going to ring Dr Cordley and tell him we've achieved some sort of breakthrough with Mother.' She swept from the bedroom.

The three men looked uneasily at each other, shuffling their feet. None of them quite knew what to say. Then Adam took the lead. 'She's right, y'know. What's past *is* past. All we have left now is Mother — with all her goodness and her faults — and the future. What we have to look at now is the cold fact that Mother sacrificed her happiness, and the rest of her life, to ensure that our lives weren't disrupted.' He had a sudden mental picture of the school Sports Day and his pregnant mother wearing a loose blue shift holding out her arms to him after he'd won the 100 yards race. He looked hard at his two brothers. 'I, for one, can accept that. I'm grateful for it.

What about you?' And he too, left the room.

Downstairs, Thalia had made tea. She looked up as Adam entered the kitchen. 'I've spoken to the doctor, he's coming round.'

'Good. It was a damn good idea of yours, Thalia, to play that particular piece of music. We all knew Mother was especially fond of it, but of course, to her it meant something very precious indeed. This is exactly the emotional twist that the doctor was talking about. We *had* to find something to reach down through all those layers of unconsciousness, something that meant enough to Mother to stir her. And, by God, I think you've done it.'

'She did move, didn't she?' Eagerness suffused her face and she clutched hold of his arm.

'Oh, she stirred. There's no doubt,' he said. 'Mother moved her head, she tried to smile.'

With joyful relief, brother and sister hugged each other unrestrainedly.

★　★　★

Dr Cordley finished his swift examination of Emma, removed his stethoscope and coiled it up in his bag together with the ophthalmoscope. He snapped the catch and straightened up. 'I do believe you've managed to penetrate the coma. Whatever it was you've done or said, you've reached her and she is responding. Now, we have to keep going and hope she continues to respond. I'll call in tomorrow.'

'Thank you, Doctor,' Adam said, 'we're very grateful to you. I'll show you out.'

'Well?' demanded Simon as Adam re-joined the other three in the kitchen.

'It's quite obvious it's worked. I, for one, am prepared to play that music over and over again — whatever feelings it gives me. It's our only link with her. If you two can't handle it, I don't bloody well care. If it's going to bring Mother back to us, then I vote we play it.' Thalia nodded vigorously. 'We'll have to take shifts though so whoever's in the room with her must project a positive attitude that she's on the mend, she's going to make it. I don't want any negative thoughts circulating round. That's all behind us.' He banged the kitchen table hard with his fist. 'From now on, the way is up.'

'Hear, hear,' Thalia responded. 'But with the look of it, we're split fifty-fifty.' She swung round to face her twin brothers. 'What do you two say?'

For a split second there was silence, then both Ian and Simon nodded.

Ian said, 'We've lost Father. Mother's all we have left. I don't want to lose her.'

'And I certainly don't,' Simon said. 'Whatever she's done is in the past. What we have now, hopefully, is Mother and the future.'

A brief smile crossed Adam's face and he drew a deep breath. 'You're saying you're with us?'

'We are.' The twins replied in unison.

'Right. We'll need a shift system. We can't expect Thalia to do it all by herself, it's not on. She needs some rest and sleep, too.' He outlined his proposal and they agreed unanimously.

Thalia sighed inwardly with relief. Since reading from the journal, there was something she very much needed to do. Whether she would be able to manage it was questionable. Whilst she had been solely nursing her mother it hadn't been possible. Now in her free time, she determined to go for it.

The journal had thrown up questions, lots and lots of questions — and she had to find the answers, preferably before her mother regained consciousness. It was a personal aspect now, not simply for her mother's benefit but for her own. She did concede it was partially selfish but since it concerned all of them, she felt justified.

After a quick lunch, which she prepared for

them all, she backed the Polo out of the garage and drove off from Alney, heading south.

Leaving the village, she kept her eye open for the nearest telephone kiosk. She couldn't use the one in Alney, there were far too many curious eyes that might notice her making a call. She couldn't risk anyone knowing what she was going to do next. Not until she had found out the answers for herself. And if what she suspected turned out to be true . . . a curious shivery feeling ran down her spine. Her mother wasn't the only one who had a secret.

She supposed she could simply drive the twenty odd miles into Leicestershire and go straight to Milo's address, the one her mother had mentioned in the journal. But that really ought to be her final destination — there was somewhere else she needed to go. Her own peace of mind must come first. Afterwards, if her suspicions were true, then would be the time to go to Milo's house.

She entered the outskirts of a small village and pulled in at the side of a red telephone kiosk. It was the right time to catch Steve at home. But after dialling, she listened in agonised suspense to the double trill endlessly repeating. She was about to replace the handset in despair when there was a click and a familiar man's voice grunted, 'Yes? Harcott Stables.'

Just the sound of his voice made Thalia feel weak. He could melt her insides even before she saw him. Oh, how well she understood what her mother had said to her. 'You will know it when it happens, Thalia.'

'Steve, it's me.'

'Darling.' All his deepest feelings came down the phone to her in that one word. She became quite light-headed with the rush of love she felt in return. 'Where are you, Thalia? Darling, are you all right?'

'Steve, please . . . I need to see you right now. I'm on my way, can I . . . is it convenient?'

'Don't be stupid, whatever time, anytime — it's always convenient.'

'Twenty minutes, then, I'll be with you.'

'God, Thalia, I've missed you like crazy.'

'I can't wait, either.' She almost ran from the kiosk, threw herself into the Polo and powered away.

Harcott Stables was about fifteen miles away and she could have driven blindfold. Steve Viceroy had been a racehorse trainer there for several years. She'd met him at Market Rasen races when, after her long delayed return to racing following her mother's recovery from the car crash, she'd been leading up one of Dickinson's steeple-chasers.

It had been a mutual attraction from the very first moment. That was going back almost a year and both had tried, unsuccessfully, to fight against their feelings.

Steve's wife had recently filed for divorce on the grounds of unreasonable behaviour, claiming his first love was his work. If she could have cited horses as co-respondents, she would have done. Steve had acknowledged she was right and had not defended the petition. He could have brought to light, if he'd so wished, the fact Monica had a lover. But he didn't. When a marriage reached that stage, it was no longer a marriage. But because of the circumstances, his love for Thalia, and her love for him, had to be kept secret.

As she drove, Thalia thought about the compelling depth of her love and could see her mother's pattern replaying. She alone knew the full extent of the journal now and was determined that she was not going to forfeit her life in the same way.

Gravel skittered away under the Polo's wheels as she braked hard in front of the kitchen door at Harcott Stables. Seconds later Steve was standing framed in the doorway — a tall, blonde man, with a wide mouth which curved into a big grin of pleasure at seeing her.

He rushed forward and yanked open the car door. His arms went around her almost lifting her from the driver's seat. 'Oh, God, Thalia, how I've missed you, darling.' His arms tightened about her as he kissed her cheeks, throat, lips. And just as she had melted on hearing his voice in the kiosk, she melted again, her knees almost buckling with the sheer delight of being close to him again. With a swift movement, he slid an arm under her thighs, swept her up and strode back into the house, kicking the door closed behind him.

In the lounge he deposited her gently on the leather chesterfield in front of the Georgian bay window. Holding up the palm of his hand in front of her face, he said, 'Now, not a word until I've poured you a stiff drink.'

'I'm driving . . . ' Thalia protested.

'One small brandy.' He grinned wickedly. 'Medicinal purposes.' He turned and thrust a balloon glass of amber liquid into her hand before pouring himself a whisky. He flung himself down beside her his arm encircling her shoulders. 'I've not heard anything from you since you phoned to say your mother was very ill.'

'I didn't want to risk another call from the

house in case I was overheard. You know how difficult it's been — with your divorce . . . '

'Tell me about it.' Steve groaned, running his fingers through his hair.

'It seems ironic going back to racing when Mother recovered from the car crash, and then meeting you. Now it seems to be old patterns replaying all over again. And you and I have been forced into this distasteful secrecy which isn't right when our feelings are as they are.'

'It won't be forever.' His arm tightened around her. 'How is your mother? I haven't dared to ring you. It's been agony waiting to hear from you.'

'This is the first chance I've had of contacting you, truly. We've been sitting by her bedside constantly. Finally, today, we've made a breakthrough. We've managed to penetrate the coma and get a response from Mother.'

'That's great news. I'm so pleased for you.'

'Thanks, but we still have a long way to go.'

'How did you manage it?'

'Well, the doctor told us we needed to keep talking to her, try to engage her emotions. Give her the will to live.'

'And so?'

'Five years ago, Mother almost died in a car crash. That's when I lost my father. At that time, I had to give up my work in racing.

You know that.' He nodded. 'I believe at that time, Mother really thought she might die. She asked me to write down secrets in a journal — things that no-one else would have ever guessed.'

'To clear her conscience, you mean?'

'Yes, something like that. Anyway, she told me I must write it down exactly as she dictated it to me, however painful that made it.' Thalia hesitated.

'Go on.'

'Believe me, Steve, it was one of the hardest things, if not *the* hardest, I have ever had to do.'

'Was it so shocking?'

'Yes.'

'Do you want to tell me?'

'Before I do, there's something I must ask you.' She tipped the brandy glass and drained it. 'I'd like another, please.'

'Hey, whoa girl, steady on. What about your driving?'

'Blow the driving. If necessary, I'll get a taxi. I need to get this off my chest.' Her hand was shaking and he stood up and looked down with concern at her face before renewing her drink.

'Just a small one.'

She smiled briefly. 'Thanks. Believe me, I do need it.'

'Yes, I can see you do.'

'Steve, before I tell you about the contents of the journal, I must ask you an important question. Your surname's Viceroy, but was your mother married twice?'

Steve's eyes widened. 'Well, that certainly wasn't what I thought you might have asked me, but yes, she was. Her first husband died and she remarried.'

'And had she already got a child, a much older one, possibly a teenager?' Thalia's hand tightened round the stem of the balloon glass as she waited for his reply.

'Yes.'

'And this other child, teenager . . . was it a boy?'

'Yes.' Steve was staring at her.

'Was his name . . . Milo, by any chance?'

His mouth dropped open. 'My God, are you psychic or something? Yes. Yes, it was Milo.'

Thalia gave a deep shuddering sigh and took a sip of brandy. 'Your mother's first husband, his surname was Kent, wasn't it?'

'That's right,' Steve said incredulously. 'How the hell did you know?'

'Woman's intuition?' Thalia's mock flippancy didn't quite come off.

'That won't wash.' Steve was shaking his head. 'Come on, Thalia, let's have the full story.'

'His address, Milo's I mean, was 85 Copse Lane, Bingham?'

'Yes.'

She gave a long broken sigh and drained the brandy. 'Then we're definitely talking about the same person.'

'I want to know how you knew all this.'

'You told me when we first met that both your parents were dead.'

'So they are.'

'You also said your half-brother had a disabled wife who lived at Bingham. There can't be many men living in Bingham whose wife's disabled and who also has a half-brother working with horses.'

'It still doesn't explain how you knew about Milo.'

'Before I say any more, Steve, I must go back to what I was telling you about Mother and that journal, five years ago.'

Impatiently, he shook his head and began to speak but she put a restraining hand on his arm. 'Please believe me, this is the right way to tell you — even if you disagree.' He shrugged resignedly.

'In essence,' Thalia continued, 'my mother, when she was a young woman, lost a child. She'd already got three young sons, my brothers, but she lost a baby. Her consultant in the hospital was — '

'Milo Kent?'

'Yes. Milo Kent.'

'Haaa . . . ' Steve nodded to himself, pursed his lips, swirling the whisky round in the tumbler.

'My mother's marriage wasn't happy and she had an affair with Milo Kent.'

Steve swallowed the whisky in a single gulp. 'Go on.'

'It was very short, I understand, only one week, but their feelings were very deep. My mother believed, still believes, they are soulmates, destined to be together.'

'History doth repeat itself,' Steve said in a low voice.

'Doesn't it just.'

They both sat and looked into one another's eyes.

'Please,' he said, 'tell me all of it.'

And so she did.

At the end he drew a shaky breath. 'Well, now we both know, don't we? Does anyone else?'

'Not as yet. But they will. I'm only part of the way through reading the journal to my brothers. That's what's bringing Mother out of her coma, so I have to go on reading it, Steve, I can't stop now. It would be impossible to stop.'

'The journal has caused her response?'

'In part. What really did it was when I played a recording of the 'Blue Danube'.'

'Haaa, their melody.'

'Yes.'

'There's something very wonderful about how the wheel has turned full circle.'

Thalia clutched his arm. 'But what about us, Steve?'

He shook his head, bewildered. 'Nothing can change the way we feel about each other.'

'My God, how can you say that? Milo was my *father*.'

'But Milo and I, we're not blood relations, Thalia.' He searched her face. 'Oh my dearest.' He pulled her tightly to him, stroking her hair. 'I should have explained. You thought we both had the same mother, didn't you?' Pressed close against his chest, she could only nod. 'Darling, Milo was adopted. Mother's first husband couldn't have children.'

Thalia felt as though a great weight lifted from her. The relief was indescribable. 'It's been a living hell trying to see a way through. And now . . . you've given me a miracle.' She lifted her face to his and their kiss seemed to last a lifetime.

When, finally, they parted, Steve said, 'So, what do we do now?'

She pushed back a loose strand of hair

from her face. 'I want to go to Milo's home. Will you come with me, please?'

'What on earth for?'

'I want to see him, speak to him if possible. If you like, get his version of what happened during that fateful week.'

He leaned across, took her empty glass and placed it beside his on the coffee table. Then he took her hands in his. 'Thalia, it's not possible. Obviously, my darling, you don't know.'

'Know what?'

'There's no gentle way of breaking this to you. My half-brother, Milo, is dead.' He watched her pupils dilate and the colour drain from her face.

'You said you had a brother,' she faltered.

'Yes, darling, *had*. I'm so very sorry, but he died five years ago.'

'What killed him?' she whispered, clutching his hand tightly.

'He had a brain tumour.'

'Oh.' She swallowed hard. 'I still need to go to his house.' She spaced the words out very deliberately.

'Why? What good would it do?'

'He may have left a diary, like Mother. Please, please take me, Steve.'

'All right, calm down girl, calm down.' He could have been talking to one of the mares in the stables, gentling her, talking softly, stroking her hand. 'If it's so important to you, of course, we'll go.'

'Now?'

'Yes, if you want to. We'll take my car. You're in no state to drive.' He stood up and put a hand beneath her elbow to support her. Together, they left the house.

Steve nosed the Range Rover swiftly through the narrow country lanes. The passing countryside was simply a blur to Thalia as she tried to come to terms with the shock of answers to questions she needed to ask. She didn't doubt what her mother had said but rather, she needed confirmation. It was this compulsion that drove her on to see where Milo had lived.

Twenty minutes later she saw the house — a large rambling property at the end of a sweeping drive down which Steve drove slowly as if knowing she needed to collect herself before they arrived.

They stood before the front door and Steve placed a supportive arm around her as he rang the doorbell. From inside the house came the deep baying of a large dog.

A plump middle-aged woman with dark curly hair showing the first few tinges of grey opened the door. 'Why, Mr Viceroy, what a nice surprise. I haven't seen you for such a long time.'

'Hello, Pearl. How are you keeping?'

'Fine, just fine.'

'And Wendy?'

Pearl nodded. 'Yes, Wendy is keeping well.'

'This is my friend, Thalia.'

'I'm very pleased to meet you.' Pearl smiled and shook Thalia's hand. 'Do come along in.'

She drew them into the hall. From behind a door came a loud snuffling. Steve saw Thalia's white strained face and smiled encouragement.

'It's all right,' he reassured. 'It's not the hound of the Baskervilles, it's only King George.'

'King . . . George?' Thalia looked at him uncertainly.

'That's right.' Pearl pushed open the door. 'He's quite harmless — a big softie, really.'

A huge, haughty head pushed itself round the door and considered them gravely.

'Oh, a Great Dane,' murmured Thalia. 'But why King George?' She put a hand out and stroked him. 'Mind you,' she added, noting his regal demeanour, 'perhaps I don't really need to ask why.'

Pearl smiled. 'There was once another Great Dane called King George who lived here . . . ' She let the words trail away.

'That's right,' put in Steve, 'a long time ago.'

Pearl smiled gratefully. 'Yes, a long time ago now.' She gathered herself. 'But come through.' She gently pushed King George aside to allow them access.

Thalia patted the big animal's firm shoulder as it gazed up at her. 'He's enormous, isn't he?'

'He belongs to Wendy,' said Pearl and indicated a wheelchair at the far end of the room facing the patio window. A woman sat in the chair, her back to them. 'I'll introduce you.'

Thalia felt her stomach give a massive lurch and cursed herself inwardly as a feeling of panic swept over her.

She had totally forgotten about Milo's wife.

15

'Wendy?' Pearl walked across the room. 'Some friends have come to see you.'

Thalia saw the blonde woman raise a right hand in acknowledgement. Panic threatened to swamp her and she hesitated. But the woman in the wheelchair simply waited with her back to them and her hand still raised.

Pearl beckoned to Thalia and took hold of Wendy's hand, dropping down on her knees at the side of the wheelchair. Reluctantly, Thalia moved towards them. She was totally unprepared for the meeting. There had been nothing in her mother's journal apart from the word, 'disabled', to describe Wendy or her handicap.

As she approached the wheelchair, Wendy turned her head a little and it took all Thalia's self-control to withhold the gasp that rose in her throat at the sight of the terribly disfigured left side. This was so much worse than she had ever imagined. But moving round to face the woman, the full horror came when she saw Wendy's whole face. The starkness between the disfigurement and the beauty was almost unbearable. She felt a flood of admiration for Milo for sparing her mother the fullest details of how Wendy really was.

Fighting back her own confused feelings, an unpleasant mixture of shame, guilt and compassion, Thalia held out her hand. 'I'm very pleased to meet you, Wendy.'

The woman in the wheelchair grunted unintelligibly.

'Wendy doesn't get many visitors. She's pleased to see you,' Pearl said as Wendy's face twisted into a caricature of a smile.

Sorrow pierced through Thalia. Floundering, unsure what to say, she seized the fact that King George had come up behind her and was now thrusting an enormous cold nose into the palm of her hand. 'This is your dog, isn't it? King George?' Wendy nodded, her smile widening. 'It's such an unusual name. There can't be any other dogs called that.'

'Wendy had Great Danes around the house before. So, when we bought this chap, we named him after the first one.' Pearl smoothed Wendy's hair affectionately.

The dog finished his inspection of Thalia and shouldered forward to lay a massive head on Wendy's shoulder, curling a long pink tongue round, licking her ear and the disfigured face. It was almost more than

Thalia could bear. The unconditional love freely given was a revelation. Wendy giggled with childlike pleasure and put her arms around the dog's neck, hugging him hard.

Steve moved to stand behind the wheelchair. 'Do you think we could open the patio window, Pearl? Maybe you'd allow me to take Wendy out and push her around the lake? King George, too, of course.'

Pearl beamed. 'That would be a lovely idea, thank you.'

'I'll leave you two girls, then,' Steve said pointedly. 'I'm sure Pearl will show you anything you want to see.' He raised an eyebrow at Pearl who nodded straight away.

'I'd be delighted to. Shall we go through to the kitchen then and I'll put the kettle on to make a drink. You can ask me anything you like.' Thalia accepted gratefully.

Impulsively, before leaving the room, she bent down and put her arms around Wendy and kissed her. 'Enjoy your trip out into the garden. I'll see you when you come back indoors.' Wendy grunted in acknowledgement and raised a hand. Thalia gripped it tightly. 'God bless you.' She was barely able to stem the tears forming at the back of her eyes.

Tactfully, Steve immediately took the brake from the wheelchair and pushed it forward. 'And I'll see you soon as well,' he whispered.

Following Pearl down the hall, self-consciously, Thalia brushed away a tear which had trickled down her cheek. 'You must think I'm being very silly,' she said when the kitchen door had closed behind them.

'Not at all. If you're not prepared for it, seeing Wendy is a shock for most people, let alone for someone who, I rather suspect, might have . . . connections?' She let the question hang in the air and busied herself filling the electric kettle.

'Can I ask you a big question to begin with, Pearl?'

'Of course.'

'Did you know a lady, or shall we say, have you heard of a lady, called Emma Wetherford?'

Pearl's hand halted as she was about to switch on the kettle. 'I've never met Emma Wetherford, but, yes — I have heard of her.'

'Through Milo?'

'Yes.' She swung round and faced Thalia. 'I thank God that Milo met Emma Wetherford when he did,' she said surprisingly. Thalia waited, at a loss now as to what the other woman was going to say.

'He was a different person after he met her,' Pearl said, looking out of the window rather dreamily now. 'Before that, he was a driven man, consumed by guilt, feeling he owed an unpayable debt not only to Wendy but to the whole world — well the world of women anyway.'

Thalia said nothing but she could identify with that feeling. It had come through so strongly from her mother as Thalia had written it down in the journal. 'And afterwards? After he met Emma?' she prompted.

Pearl smiled. 'He regained his own self-respect — lost an enormous load of guilt, became far more relaxed — he allowed himself to enjoy life again. Of course, this benefitted Wendy, too.'

'Yes, I can see it would.'

'So, yes,' Pearl switched on the kettle, 'I do have a lot to thank Emma Wetherford for. But although she gave him such gifts for himself, which he sorely needed, I must admit, there was a price to be paid.'

'Isn't there always?'

'Yes. There's no denying Milo grieved very much for Emma. But it was not to be. On the sane and conscious level he knew that but on that other level we all have, he bled daily for her.'

'As deep as that?'

'Yes.' Now it was Pearl's turn to ask a question. 'Just who are you, Thalia? What connection did you have with Milo? If you'd rather not say, I understand.'

The silence lengthened as she sought for the right words and found none. In desperation, she blurted out, 'The reason I have come ... did Milo keep a diary? Or anything at all in writing that referred to the period of time when he met Emma Wetherford? You see,' she rushed on, 'I didn't know Milo had died. I thought coming here today, I was going to meet him, so that I could ask face to face, find out the truth.'

Pearl started to shake her head. 'No. He kept no diary.' Thalia felt the hope within her flicker and die.

'Well, it was a long shot,' she said dejectedly. 'But there were some things that I desperately needed to, well, not really find out but rather, have confirmed.'

'Could you not answer my question? What connection have *you* with Milo?'

Thalia gripped the edge of the kitchen table and dredged up the courage, licking her lips that felt suddenly dry and stiff. 'Emma Wetherford was Milo's mistress.' She hardly dared look at Pearl but the woman was nodding.

'I know.'

Emboldened by the woman's open acceptance, she said, 'I am Emma Wetherford's daughter.'

'Haaaa,' Pearl gave a gusty sigh and sat down very suddenly on the kitchen chair. 'I wondered,' she murmured. 'Yes, I wondered . . . ' She stared hard at Thalia. 'You see, my dear,' she reached across and placed her hand over Thalia's where it lay on the kitchen table, 'when I look at you — I see Milo. You have Milo's eyes. You are his daughter — aren't you?'

Thalia nodded.

Both women sat silently looking at each other, both trying to adjust to the situation.

Then Thalia, with a flash of inspiration, said, 'I'm out of order, I know, but you loved him, too, didn't you?'

Pearl's eyes lowered and she bit her lip. 'Very much.'

A bond seemed to stretch between them that had not been there before.

'I think,' said Thalia, 'that you are a very generous and warm-hearted woman to speak so highly of my mother, knowing that she and Milo were lovers.'

'They were more than lovers,' Pearl said simply. 'They were the two halves of each other.'

For a few moments, Thalia was unable to speak for emotion, but when she had composed herself somewhat she said, 'I would love to see a photograph of Milo, of my *father*.'

'Certainly.' Pearl rose. 'Come up to his room.' She led Thalia upstairs and down the landing to a room whose window overlooked the lake. Thalia went and leaned on the wide window ledge. Outside, she could see the figure of Steve and the majestic long strides of King George walking at the side of him as he took Wendy in her wheelchair around the perimeter of the lake.

'Here we are.' Pearl had produced a photograph album. 'This one's my favourite.'

She flicked over a few pages and picked a snapshot of Milo holding a large plant pot from which bloomed a magnificent mauve-tinged orchid. He looked very youthful, very happy. Thalia gazed at it hungrily.

'Of course, it was taken before Wendy's accident. They were blissfully happy together, initially.'

'I'm sure they were. Do you know how he described her to my mother?'

Pearl shook her head. 'Tell me, please.'

'He said she was a carefree, blonde goddess of a girl — vitally alive.'

'Oh, how wonderful to describe someone like that, and truly mean it.'

Thalia's heart went out to her. 'You are the most generous-spirited woman I have ever come across.'

'I'm afraid,' Pearl looked down at her

hands, 'I haven't been quite open, honest, with you. A long time after Emma had gone, I and Milo . . . comforted each other.' She looked hesitantly at Thalia, unsure of the girl's reactions.

'I'm very glad. You both needed each other.'

'Thank you for your understanding.' Relief showed clearly in her eyes. 'It certainly seemed right for us to care for each other. But don't forget, Thalia, there was Wendy. She needed *both* of us and it formed a necessary bridge between Milo and me.'

'Yes, I can see that it would. But I'm still pleased to know you brought him some happiness.'

'Thank you.' Embarrassed, Pearl walked across and looked out of the window.

Thalia let her gaze drop once more to the photograph album. 'Did Milo know? About me?'

'No. But I'm sure he does now, wherever he is.'

Thalia looked up. 'You really believe that?'

'Yes, I do.'

'So does my mother. Emma.'

'And do you, Thalia?'

'I'm not sure. I'd like to. But it hasn't been proved scientifically has it?'

'How can it be? The whole concept of life,

love's continuance is based on faith, that's the beauty of it. If we knew for certain — that would change the world.'

'It's already starting to change — people's awareness, consciousness — is expanding, that's a fact.'

Pearl laughed softly. 'If you know that, then you also know love survives.' She lifted a hand and waved to Wendy through the window. 'But we're getting a little deep.' She turned and walked over to Thalia. 'Look, I tell you what, I'd be pleased to let you borrow the photograph album, if you promise to return it.'

'Thanks, I'd love to spend time looking through it.'

'Settled, then. You take the album back with you. And I'm sure if there is a particular photograph of Milo that you would like to keep, he'd like you to have it.'

'You're very kind. I do appreciate it . . . ' Thalia felt emotion well up inside her. 'I'm sure I shall know the right one when I come to it.'

'Thalia,' Pearl hesitated, 'I was withholding certain information when I said Milo didn't keep a diary.'

Thalia felt her heart suddenly start to race. 'He did?'

'No, but he did make a tape of that time

when he met Emma Wetherford. He put everything down on it. He allowed me to listen to it, with him,' she was twisting her hands now in acute embarrassment, 'but it was a long time afterwards.'

Thalia said nothing, her sympathy going out to this woman.

'Milo left the tape with me in case at any time your mother were to come here.'

Thalia frowned. 'But he could have posted it.'

Pearl shook her head. 'His words were, 'I don't want to compromise Emma, in any way.''

Thalia heard again her mother's words just as she herself had written them down. 'Yes,' she said slowly, 'I can understand he would say that.'

'But if your mother were to come here — ask about him — well, that would be different.' Pearl went to a roll-top desk in the corner and turned the key in one of the drawers. Right at the back, wrapped in soft chamois leather was a small package. She drew it out. 'This is for you. With Milo's love.'

'I have already found the answers, the information, I was looking for,' Thalia said in a low voice, reaching out with trembling fingers to take the package. 'But this is going to be another one of those bridges — this time between Milo and my mother.' Seeing the bewilderment in Pearl's eyes, she quickly told her of Emma's illness.

'I sincerely hope she recovers.' Pearl squeezed her hand.

Steve's voice, calling from downstairs, broke into their conversation.

'Come along,' Pearl walked purposefully towards the stairs, 'it's a long time since I put that kettle on. We'll have to re-boil it for coffee.'

Thalia laughed. 'Absolutely.'

The two women smiled at each other, linked arms and together they came down the wide staircase.

16

Steve, keeping his eyes on the road as he drove the Range Rover back to Harcott Stables and sensing Thalia's need for space, had refrained, with difficulty, from asking any questions. But after parking the car and turning off the engine, he twisted in his seat and looked at her. 'Well, did you find the answers to your questions?'

'Hmmmm,' she nodded, fingering the small package in her pocket that Pearl had given her. The larger one she had placed on her lap. She showed him. 'Pearl said I might bring this back with me so that I could take my time looking at it. It's the photograph album.'

He nodded. 'Yes, I recognise it. The album's been in the family for donkey's years.'

'She said I could choose one to keep.'

'One?'

'Oh, a photograph of Milo.' Thalia had to remind herself Steve was still in the dark about her conversation with Pearl.

'To give to your mother, presumably?'

Not wishing to tell an outright lie, she said, 'I'm sure she'd like to see it, if . . .

when . . . we can pull her round completely from the coma.'

Steve turned the car keys round and round in his strong fingers. Without looking at her, he said, 'Are you coming in?'

'Would you mind awfully if I don't?'

'No, not if you don't want to,' he said.

'I'd like some time by myself, if you don't mind. I need to, well, adjust I suppose, to what Pearl's been telling me.'

'Of course.'

They stepped from the Range Rover and Thalia fished her own car keys from her shoulder-bag.

'Thalia.' He caught her arm as she was unlocking the Polo. 'Please ring me. I love you, for God's sake. Don't leave it like this — in the air. I can't stand it. Promise you'll ring.'

She gulped and nodded. 'I promise. But right now, I have to get back, see how Mother is.'

'I do understand,' Steve said.

She felt a jolt at those so familiar words — spoken this time by the man she loved. Impulsively, she threw her arms round his neck, drew his head down and kissed him on the lips. 'Bless you, Steve, for your understanding. I promise I'll give you a ring. But now I'm going.' She slid behind the wheel, started the engine and drove the Polo away very fast. Glancing in her rear view mirror, she saw him still standing looking after the car. He raised a forlorn hand just a few inches and let his hand drop again.

She choked back a sob and pushed her right foot down hard on the accelerator. What a bloody mess, she thought, if only we were both free. The main thing, she had wanted to say to Steve — the most important one — had after all, remained unsaid.

Thalia bit her lip in impotent frustration. It would have to wait now. Well, she supposed it could for a short time, whilst she came to terms with the facts she had learned this afternoon. Right now, there was too much to get her head round. She felt dazed by the emotional trauma.

Putting her hand into her pocket she fingered the edge of the small package Pearl had given her. This could well prove the complete breakthrough they all hoped and longed for.

Feeling a strong urge to get back she brought her wandering thoughts into focussed concentration upon her driving. It would never do to daydream and have a smash.

She swung in between the twin lions and pulled up outside the front door. Letting herself in, she stood for a moment or two in the hall listening. She had expected to hear the strains of the 'Blue Danube' floating down the staircase from her mother's bedroom, as it had been playing endlessly since early morning.

Strangely, now, the house was totally silent. Dropping the album and package on the hall table, she raced up the stairs, anxiety running rife through her. What had happened whilst she'd been away? Oh God, surely . . . surely not . . . she burst in through the door of her mother's bedroom — and stopped.

She let the door close behind her and slumped back against it as her knees suddenly turned to water.

Her three brothers were sitting grouped round the head of the bed. Adam was holding his mother's hand. Thalia could see her mother's eyes. They were wide open.

Ian jumped up as Thalia entered the room. He caught her hand. 'Isn't it marvellous, Sis? Mother's come out of the coma.'

'Mother, oh Mother!' She was across the room and hugging her fiercely.

'Steady on, kiddo.' Simon patted her shoulder. 'You'll smother Mother.' And light-headed with giddy relief, they all giggled like children at the stupidity of the remark.

'Thank God you've come round, Mother. But I should have been here.' Thalia clenched her fists at her own inadequacy.

'It's all right, darling,' Emma said in a weak voice.

'We played the 'Blue Danube' again,' said Adam. 'Mother continued to respond so we kept on playing it. And about half an hour ago,' he bent and kissed Emma with an uprush of love, 'she surfaced.' And they all burst out laughing again.

'Now you're back with us,' Thalia was still hugging her mother as though she would never let go, 'you're going to be looked after. We shall all make jolly sure of that. Do you know, we thought we'd lost you?'

'Did you, darling?'

'Yes, we did. And it was bloody awful. So if you've got any more thoughts in that direction,' Thalia said, in mock anger, 'forget it. You're back here now, with us. And this is where you're staying.'

'Yes,' Emma murmured weakly, 'but I *was* tempted to stay. It was so very beautiful . . . '

There was a sudden strained silence in the room. The three men looked warily at one another, uncomprehendingly.

Thalia looked at her mother. 'When you're strong, if you wish, I'd love you to tell me about . . . where you've been.'

There was a sudden strange bond of sensitivity between the two women that seemed to totally exclude the men.

Adam cleared his throat. 'Well, now you're back, Thalia, I'm going to go down and phone Dr Cordley.'

She turned to face him. 'You haven't told him yet?'

'No, we were all so absolutely thrilled beyond belief when Mother actually started to come round, we just stayed with her.'

'We didn't want to leave her,' Ian put in.

'Not likely,' added Simon.

'Anyway, I'm going to ring now.'

'We'll come with you,' the twins said.

'What about a cup of tea, Mother?' Simon asked, bending over and kissing her cheek. 'I bet you could do with one, eh?'

'You're a good boy,' Emma murmured drowsily, 'a cup of tea would be lovely.'

'Yes, Ma'am,' Ian raised a hand to his temple in mock salute, 'five minutes.'

The doctor seemed genuinely delighted when he came round shortly afterwards. 'I never cease to marvel at miracles with my patients,' he said.

'Any instructions, Doctor?' Simon enquired.

'Take things very, very gently. Only light nourishment to begin with, and above all, plenty of rest — no strain of any sort.' They nodded. 'Your mother will need a lot of care,' the doctor looked at Thalia, 'but I know she will get it.'

'Of course.'

'And you should see a slight improvement each day that goes past. But don't let her be in too much of a hurry. It's most definitely bed-rest for the next few days.'

'Very well.' Thalia opened the door as she spoke. 'You can rely on me, Dr. Cordley.'

He stepped outside into the autumn sunshine. 'I'm very pleased for you all.' He gave a rare smile. 'Don't forget, call me if you need to, otherwise, I'll pop in sometime tomorrow to check on her progress.'

'Thank you, we're all very grateful.'

The doctor was about to get into his car when he stopped and looked wonderingly at Thalia. 'Whatever it was that roused your mother, it must have been something pretty important to her, emotionally.'

'It was,' Thalia said simply, 'the most important thing — love.'

He compressed his lips in satisfaction and nodded. 'It usually is. Love has miraculous powers, far greater than medical science.'

Emma went back into the house and closed the door. On the hall chest was the photograph album and the package. She hesitated for a moment, uncertainly, then came to a decision.

The whole point of playing the tape had

been to bring her mother out of the coma. Now that was no longer required. But before her brothers enquired too deeply about the album, she felt that Emma should see it first, privately.

She picked up the tape. What should she do about it? Tried to think what Milo himself would have wanted, since it was his thoughts that were recorded upon it. Pearl had said Milo hadn't wanted to compromise Emma by sending it — but he had wanted it to be available should Emma herself wish to approach him. There had been no mention of her. Of course there hadn't. Milo hadn't known Emma was pregnant with his child. At that point, the question ceased to exist. The tape was Emma's alone. It had nothing to do with Thalia personally, so she would lock it away together with the album in the desk in her bedroom and when Emma was a little stronger, that would be the time to present both items to her.

She could only pray that they would have a positive effect on her mother's healing and perhaps be the final step towards her complete recovery.

Resolutely, she gathered the items up, went swiftly upstairs to her room and locked them away in the drawer in her desk.

Within three days, Emma was sitting up and looking much more her normal self. She was still very weak but definitely on the mend. On the third morning, she greeted Thalia's arrival with her breakfast tray with increased interest.

'Darling, scrambled egg, lovely. I feel I could tackle some food this morning. Do you know, I'm a little bit hungry for the first time.'

'That's great news.' Thalia placed the tray on the bed and kissed her mother before plumping the pillows. Drawing up a chair by the bed, she chatted whilst Emma tucked in with evident pleasure to the nourishing hot food, a dainty crustless square of toast spread with marmite and topped with fluffy scrambled egg.

When Emma had finished eating, Thalia said, 'There's plenty more toast in the kitchen, if you'd like some more.'

'No, that was delicious but I've had sufficient.' She sipped at the misted glass of chilled orange juice. Already there was a pink flush of returning health and strength in her cheeks. Thalia felt her heart lift.

'You know you gave us such a fright, Mother, when you went under.'

'Did I, darling?'

'Yes. We thought we were going to lose you.'

Emma was silent for a moment, tracing a pattern in the mist on the side of the glass. 'It was a wonderful place . . . where I went to, Thalia,' she murmured.

'Where was it?' Thalia's voice had dropped to almost a whisper although she couldn't have said why.

'I can't tell you', Emma continued. 'All I know is, the peace was absolute. It was a place filled with love.' The tonal quality of her voice altered significantly. 'And Milo was there . . . '

Thalia caught her breath, 'Milo?'

'Yes, darling, Milo.' Her mother's eyes had a faraway look in them now, very wistful. 'I met him again, in that lovely place. I wanted to stay so very much.' Emma was looking into the middle distance now, seeing nothing. Her face seemed to glow with inner light, become young and beautiful once more. 'Everything was timeless, eternal . . . '

Thalia reached for her mother's hand, cradled it gently between her own. 'You were in a deep coma . . . '

'And you think I was hallucinating, my darling?'

'It's possible you were . . . '

'No, no. It all seemed very real to me.'

'But you chose to come back to us.'

'I heard your voice, Thalia, you spoke to me.'

Thalia trembled a little. 'I did? What did I say?'

'You said, 'The music is making contact', and I heard the 'Blue Danube' playing far away.' Emma's voice was very soft now. 'I was back in time, a very long way back — twenty-eight years ago, to the afternoon when you were conceived.

'I had been in an emotional desert for so long with Charles. I'd not known happiness and love for years — until I met Milo. My darling, he brought me such exquisite joy and happiness. We laughed and loved and played, we were light-hearted, it was another world.

Thalia waited, afraid to break into the magic bubble that seemed to surround her mother.

'Have you ever wondered why I chose the name, Thalia, for you darling?'

'No. Is there a special reason?'

Emma smiled, 'Oh yes. I named you after the muse of humour, because that was what Milo represented to me, happiness — unbounded, sublime happiness.'

17

Mother and daughter, cheeks pressed together, hugged each other tightly.

Thalia, her voice choked with emotion, said, 'I'm very blessed. To be given life by parents that loved each other so much.'

Her mother lifted a hand and gently brushed away the tears running down Thalia's face. 'We were all three of us very blessed — we still are.'

'Oh, how I wish I'd known my father.'

'My darling, we are still all together, he hasn't gone. The place where he is now, it's timeless, simply a loving thought away, that's all.'

'I wish,' Thalia bent her head guiltily, 'that I could believe . . . '

'I know, I know.' Emma kissed her daughter with loving compassion. 'When you've experienced it, doubt does not exist. But to have faith without first experiencing, shall we say, proof, is a courageous thing.'

'I just wish I could picture his face. You know, hold him close in that way. Oh! Wait . . . wait . . . ' Thalia jumped to her feet. 'Of course, I've just remembered, there's the photograph album.'

She dashed from the room. Returning a few moments later, she placed a photograph album down on the bedclothes.

'Open it, Mother. I've kept it safely locked away in my desk for the last three days so that no-one else would accidentally come across it. I wanted you to see it first.'

Emma stared at her. 'This is Milo's?'

Thalia nodded.

Emma took a deep breath and opened the album.

★ ★ ★

The first few photographs were of Milo's mother and father. The very first one was of their wedding day.

'It's so strange,' Thalia said, 'to think they were my grandparents.' The two women pored over them. Several honeymoon snaps followed. 'They were very much in love, weren't they?'

Someone had taken a picture that showed Milo's father standing in a punt at Cambridge, legs slightly straddled as he braced himself, holding the pole rigid whilst reaching out to take the hand of his new bride. She smiled down at him with trusting adoration as she prepared to step aboard.

Emma pointed out one that showed the two hand-in-hand, standing beside the walls of an old castle perched on a cliff.

The wind lifted the woman's hair whilst her husband attempted to prevent her scarf from blowing away. The woman's head was thrown back and she was laughing up at him.

'They look so happy together,' she said wistfully. 'Happiness is such a precious thing.'

Thalia squeezed her hand. 'Look at these, Mother.'

She turned the page over to reveal photographs of a baby, obviously Milo, through the varying stages of babyhood, infancy through junior school, resplendent in short trousers and striped school cap, to finally, mortar board and scroll as he graduated from University.

'I'm so glad you brought the album for me to look at.' Emma touched Milo's face lovingly on the last photograph. 'It gives such a marvellous background to my memories of him.'

She sighed and turned over to the following photographs. These were of a wedding.

Thalia bent forward to read the caption, 'Wendy and me on our wedding day.' Apprehensively, she flashed a quick glance at her mother's face but Emma was openly looking at it with great interest.

'Yes, he was so right,' she murmured half to herself, 'the way he described Wendy.'

Thalia looked back at the photograph and saw exactly what her mother meant. Brides were supposed to look radiant, but this girl looked vitally alive, positively exhilarated and above all very beautiful.

The following snaps only served to emphasise this. There were single ones of Wendy as she was caught playing tennis, returning a backhand, swinging the racquet high ready to serve, looking stunning in short, white, pleated skirt with her long, golden hair caught back by a scarlet band. One taken where she was stretched out on a beach wearing a black bathing suit, reaching forwards, pointing towards a ship that could just be discerned far out to sea.

There were snaps of Milo, too. One had him holding aloft a silver trophy in one hand and an orchid in the other. Another showed him trundling a wheelbarrow down the garden path, complete with muddy wellingtons, raising a cheery hand to the camera, laughing good naturedly at being caught at an inopportune moment.

And then they came to one of Milo, by himself, astride a black horse. Emma suddenly broke down and began to sob — quiet, deep sobs that seemed to come from

248

the very heart of her.

'Mother,' Thalia enfolded her in loving arms, 'if it's so upsetting, we won't look at the album anymore.'

'No, no.' With an effort, Emma wiped her eyes. 'I want to, really I do. But that horse he's riding, that's Ross.'

'You mean when you went on the beach ride with him?'

'Yes, that's the one.'

For long minutes Emma gazed down at the photograph before she could bring herself to turn the page. One enlargement stood out — again of Milo, this time cupping a Great Dane's head between his hands and looking down at it with immense fondness. Instantly, Thalia knew this was 'her' photograph. This was the one meant for her.

She in turn, could feel sobs welling up from deep inside, sadness for the father she had never known until now — when it was too late to feel the touch of his hand, the affection of his kiss on her cheek. Although she hadn't sobbed openly, Emma looked across with compassion at her daughter as if sensing that she, too, had experienced a bonding with this man.

Slowly now, they turned the last pages. These were family groups and once again pictures of a baby dressed in a blue romper suit struggling to stand, grinning gummily at the camera, being pushed in a pushchair round a lake and excitedly pointing with a plump, dimpled, little hand to a flotilla of ducks that were approaching.

More snaps followed his progress from first day at school through to senior school and later, dressed in jodhpurs and hard hat, about to mount a large chestnut horse. There had been no captions beneath the baby photographs, only the year, but for the first time beneath this one, it read, 'My brother, Steve — achieving his ambitions.'

Before either of the women could comment, the bedroom door opened and Thalia's three brothers appeared. Thalia started guiltily. It was too late to try to hide the album. But she need not have worried.

Emma reached out her hands to the men. 'I want to show you something, my darlings. Thalia has been given a photograph album to show me. And I want to share it with you all.'

Ian bent over the bed and picked it up. 'Snapshots, eh? Who are they?' And then he stiffened as he read Milo's name. 'Oh.'

The one word expressed the whole of his disapproval and Thalia felt her hands clench. 'No strain', the doctor had said. She desperately tried to make eye contact with Ian to mutely beg that he didn't upset their mother at this stage of her recovery. But with great restraint, Ian handed back the album.

'Of course, Mother,' he said, 'I can understand you wishing to see it.'

Thalia's mouth dropped open in surprise. She hadn't expected him to be so magnanimous.

'Here, let me have a look.' Adam held out his hand. Simon leaned over Adam's shoulder as his eldest brother turned the pages.

Adam flicked through and stopped, arrested by the picture of Milo and the dog. 'Well, I must say, he looks a pretty decent sort of a bloke.'

'I was thinking the same thing myself,' Simon said.

Thalia sneaked a glance at her mother who returned it and they smiled secretly together.

Ian was looking very serious now. 'I suppose,' he said, 'That in a way, we should be grateful to this . . . Milo.' The others looked at him and waited. 'If it hadn't been for him, there'd have been no journal for Thalia to read from. And we wouldn't have achieved a breakthrough with Mother.'

'That's right,' agreed Simon. 'So really, he's done us a favour.'

Emma looked from one to the other of her sons. 'Has Thalia finished reading you the journal?'

'No, not yet.' Thalia shook her head. 'I'd reached the piece about the ... log cabin ... ' She hesitated, hardly daring to put her thoughts into words because of the delicacy of the situation. 'But it's where we found the piece about the 'Blue Danube'. And that's why we played it.'

'Right.' Emma closed the album. 'What I would like you to do, Thalia, if you would be so good, please, is to read your brothers the final part of my journal.'

Thalia caught her breath. 'You're quite sure about this?'

'Oh yes. I am *very* sure. Half a secret revealed is no good. It must be the whole truth. I'm not prepared to live a lie anymore.'

Ian looked about to protest but Adam waved him down. 'If it's what Mother wants,' he said firmly, 'then we go along with it. Thalia, perhaps you would fetch the journal whilst we get seated ready to listen?'

PART SIX

1954

18

I sat on the York train as it swayed and rattled along, taking me back to the life I did not want. My head, my heart, indeed my soul, I had left behind in the log cabin at Sandsend. They were forever the property of my Milo.

These last few days had been a joyous heavenly experience. But life exacted a price. Interaction with other human beings frequently included duty. When duty combined with love, there was never any question of the way to go. It was explicit, brooking no argument.

Every fibre of me yearned to turn the train around, return to Sandsend and Milo. But duty stood before me, beckoning gently, not demanding but nevertheless, impossible to refuse.

Ahead of me at home waited my three young sons and even as I yearned to return to Milo, the mother in me yearned to be with my children, to nurture them, love them, bring them up to be independent adults. There was never any question of putting my own wants before theirs. It was doubly impossible because Milo was also bound by the gossamer thin yet stronger than steel bonds of love and duty to his handicapped wife. And no way would I even try to persuade him otherwise. Both of us knew that the few days we had shared would, in all probability, be the only ones spent together during our lifetime. We each needed to be strong for the other.

We had to break apart that beautiful complete eggshell, separate two hands from the face of life's clock and return to our respective families. There would be intense grieving for both of us at this parting and indeed, I felt my heart had been cut out.

But trickling in, like the sweet melted butterscotch of the afterglow of our loving, was the healing balm of knowing that one day, somewhere, our life together would begin again — we were soulmates, this was not the end.

It was to this surety, emanating from my solar plexus, cocooning me in the warmth of its assurance, that I clung as a drowning man to a plank of wood, as the train bore me ever onwards, farther and farther away from Milo.

*   *   *

Initially, when I reached home I felt the joy of rediscovering the unconditional love poured out by my twin boys as they squeaked their delight and welcomed me home again. But when the euphoria of being back with them once more had settled down into the normal routine of life, which in my case happened to be two or three days, my longing for Milo pained me so much I could scarcely bear it. There was a great, gaping hole where my heart should have been. But I forced myself to think of the twins and their future. I reminded myself, sometimes hourly, of the solemn promise made as I journeyed north less than two weeks ago. And it helped, a little.

★ ★ ★

It was nearing the end of the twins' last week at school before the start of their half-term holiday when I approached Charles on the subject of our going away together as a family for a few days holiday. I desperately needed to re-establish my roots within the home circle. It was something that must be done or I would not survive.

To my surprise, Charles had had second thoughts about taking time off from the business.

'As a matter of fact,' he said, one night shortly after I had returned home, 'I've been giving it some thought and a few days away would do the boys the world of good.'

I was very pleased by his decision but it didn't escape my notice that he'd said it would do the boys good, he had not mentioned how things stood between us. I pushed it to the back of my mind.

Another thought, like a new shoot pushing through the soil, was refusing to stop growing and I was uneasy in the extreme. If what I suspected were true, I would need to do something about it quickly. My breasts had become very sore.

It would entail being thoroughly deceitful — something I abhorred. At this point, I began to dislike myself very much indeed.

'I anticipated,' Charles said, 'that you'd have no objections, so I've gone ahead and rented us a cottage in Yorkshire for a week. I haven't told the boys yet. Obviously, I needed your . . . comments.' He hesitated over the last word. Not permission, approval or agreement — simply, *comments*. I would have given an angry retort but the need for deceit overcame my natural indignation at the way he was riding roughshod over me.

'Whatever you say, Charles,' I said demurely, whilst inside anger raged.

Predictably, the next morning, when I told the twins, they yelled and danced in glee at the thought of the forthcoming holiday.

But that was as nothing to their delight as I collected them from infant school after breaking up early on Friday afternoon. The sight of their happy faces was very soothing to the hurt and grief still sharply piercing through me. By now I knew what I'd suspected was fact. I had to follow through with my distasteful plan. It was no longer just a possibility, it must be carried out.

★ ★ ★

The cottage was pure chocolate box, perched on the very edge of a moor on the outskirts of a little village. It afforded the twins all the freedom, fresh air and scope that two young boys needed. But it was small. And as we explored the interior on that first morning, inside I cheered along with the boys when I discovered that there were only two bedrooms, one boasting bunk beds for the twins — the other containing a double bed.

Charles did not seem to find the prospect unattractive. It seemed he was anticipating a reconciliation whilst I, too, was quite prepared to go along with that because it fitted in with my underhanded plan.

For the first couple of days we walked the

moor during the day and were so tired by bedtime that we all slept soundly from the moment we climbed into bed.

But this could not continue.

Whilst I was becoming more relaxed, enjoying my sons' company and revelling in their happiness, I also had to force myself to become more and more affectionate towards Charles. I hated being so two-faced but I needed to have intercourse with him as soon as possible.

When Charles actually did make love to me, it was very weird but I found I could detach myself from my true feelings and stand objectively to one side. I gave a good performance of pretending to enjoy his attentions but this was from necessity, not want — and certainly not from love.

When we returned home at the end of the week ready for the twins to restart their school term, I rejoiced that I now had the perfect alibi. I needed one because as I had discovered very quickly after returning from Sandsend, I was pregnant. Charles, of course, would undoubtedly assume the child I was carrying to be his.

But it wasn't — it was Milo's.

★　★　★

I told no-one, delighting in my precious secret, hugging it close to me. I didn't need a doctor to confirm that I was an expectant mother but began, instead, mentally ticking off the weeks.

The date for my monthly period came and went and only after six weeks, when I began to feel nauseous, did I go to see the doctor.

After his examination, I finished dressing behind the screen and went to sit in front of the familiar mahogany desk. Dr Cordley finished meticulously drying his hands and picked up his pen, making an entry on my medical notes that were lying on the desk.

'Well, Mrs Wetherford.' He placed the fountain pen down with great deliberation. 'I have the feeling you don't really need me to tell you the happy news.' His eyes twinkled across at me. 'Am I right?'

I nodded, suddenly, joyously speechless.

'Congratulations, it's the best possible thing that could happen.' He leaned across the wide desk and pumped my hand.

But in the midst of my jubilation, a cold fear shivered its way down my spine. 'Doctor, my last baby, you know, I had a miscarriage . . . ' I had no need to say anything further, the query was in my voice and he knew immediately what I was afraid of.

'It doesn't follow, Mrs Wetherford, that

you'll have another miscarriage. Don't forget, you've already successfully carried three babies to full term.'

I nodded, reassured. The thought of losing this baby was too dreadful to contemplate. This was my one tenable link with my beloved Milo. If I could not have him at least I would have his child, a small part of him — one that would be with me, God willing, for the rest of my days. Then I asked the question to which I already knew the answer. 'How far gone am I?'

'A good six weeks.'

My heart soared with joy. Six weeks ago, I had been in a log cabin with Milo at Sandsend, not a holiday cottage in Yorkshire with Charles.

*　★　*

Later that evening, when the twins were tucked up snugly in bed, I read them a bedtime story, kissed them goodnight and went downstairs to tell Charles I was pregnant. I wondered what his reaction would be but by now I was impervious to whatever response he gave. It was predictable.

Carefully setting down his half-finished glass of whisky, he raised his eyebrows and said ruefully, 'Holidays, hmmm, one of the pitfalls . . . I suppose we asked for it.' There were no words of tender delight or congratulations, just a stoic acceptance of a straightforward case of cause and effect. Instead of being desperately upset as I had been on that last occasion when I'd told Charles I was pregnant, this time I was totally indifferent. Then he compounded that indifference.

'Still, I dare say, at least you're pleased about it.'

All I felt for him then was a wave of pity that his heart should be so hard and unfeeling when instead he should have been elated and filled with happiness.

The next day, when the twins had been safely deposited at school and Charles was at business, I sat down and thought very hard about whether I should write a letter to tell Milo.

Selfishly, I was bursting to give him the marvellous news that he was to be a father. But after a great deal of thought, I decided it would be too incredibly cruel. He had lost his only chance of raising a family with Wendy. I could not bear to turn a knife in that old wound.

But I felt the need to make some kind of symbolic gesture to give thanks for the baby who had been given to us both.

After much deliberation, I decided upon, what was to me, the most symbolic thing that had resulted in the conception of this new life through my union with Milo.

I went into Nottingham and bought a recording of Strauss's 'Blue Danube'.

After lunch, I went upstairs and changed, putting on my blue dress. As I fastened each of the buttons, I thought of Milo's tender touch as he had taken each button in his fingers and, one by one, undone them. I had not worn the dress since. Then I sat before the dressing table and brushed my long auburn hair until it rippled like silk. Finally, I sprayed on a fine mist of L'Aimant perfume. I had used the same perfume that day, six weeks ago, before I'd gone to the log cabin.

Then I went downstairs and played the recording of the 'Blue Danube'.

I stood looking through the long French windows that led out across the patio and lawn and let the music take me back to that afternoon in the log cabin.

It had changed my life.

When I returned home I'd buried my true emotions deep inside. But as the glorious music rose and fell, swirled and filled the room, I felt those emotions begin to rise — it was like a lorry shedding a load of bricks straight into my solar plexus.

I rushed to the bathroom, retched and retched, clawing at my hair, feeling the wild tears inside fighting to get out.

I collapsed onto the settee as the last few bars of the 'Blue Danube' played away into silence.

Our baby would be born in seven months' time. If I did not take a strong hold upon myself, it was more than possible I would lose it.

There was a stark choice before me now, either I became strong or I cracked up. If I cracked up, I would undoubtedly lose this precious baby and if that happened then I, too, might as well be dead. I would have lost Milo twice.

So, I chose the way forward — the hard way.

Now I would live — for my three sons and for Milo's baby.

PART SEVEN

1983

19

Thalia came to the end of Emma's journal and closed the book.

There was shocked silence in the bedroom. Even before she lifted her head, she could feel her three brothers staring at her. She knew what turmoil they must be going through and what they must be thinking: 'She isn't our full sister but a half-sister.'

'The hair colouring,' Adam said finally, 'that should have told us.' Thalia involuntarily put up a hand to her long, blonde hair.

'I don't know,' Simon said, frowning heavily, 'after all, Mother's auburn.' He switched a bewildered gaze between Emma and Thalia as he considered it.

'Not so,' Ian said decisively. 'Genetics. The colour comes from the dominant chromosome, usually the male side, not the female.'

'I really don't know why you're going on about the colour of Thalia's hair,' Emma said. 'All that need concern you is that you are all *my* children. That is sufficient.' Her voice held a note of reprimand in it which, despite being adults, the child-self within them acknowledged as authority and backed off.

'Did you ever tell Father?' Ian queried.

'No. I never did.'

'Don't you think you should have done?'

Emma spread her hands. 'That, of course, my darlings, was where I had to be horridly deceitful. Don't forget, I also lost a lot of my own self-respect and integrity. It was the price I paid. But it was to safeguard your sister and yourselves.

'However, your father's dead now, and my revealing what should be revealed won't hurt him. I didn't want to go to my death still keeping the secret. I would prefer to die with a clear conscience.'

The three men looked at each other. 'We really thought we were going to lose you, Mother,' Simon said. The others nodded.

'You will one day, darlings,' Emma said softly, 'it's inevitable. But just as inevitable, is the fact we shall all be together again, at some point in the future.'

Ian shuffled uncomfortably. 'I think you're getting a bit too deep for me, Mother.'

Emma laughed. 'Men,' she said disparagingly, but without rancour. 'You are so reluctant to acknowledge your feminine qualities, such as intuition. You do have them, you know. It is not weakness, but strength.'

'Maybe Strauss knew all about his feminine qualities,' Adam said. 'Perhaps he drew on them when he wrote the 'Blue Danube'.'

'Quite likely,' Emma agreed.

They were skirting around in the aftermath of the bombshell and they all knew it. But it was going to take time to balance up their thoughts and feelings about it.

Simon stood up and went over to kiss his mother. 'We have to get back to the business. We'll leave you with Thalia now and we'll be back about teatime.'

He leaned forward and caught Thalia's face between his two hands, kissing her forehead. 'Make sure you look after our mother, Sis,' he said and walked out.

The other two, taking his lead, kissed Emma before following him. At the door Adam turned round and looked back at Thalia. 'You've always been my kid sister.'

Ian nodded in agreement then added for them all, 'So what's new?'

As the door closed behind them, Thalia said with great relief, 'It's going to be all right, Mother. I think they've accepted it.'

'Give them time, it's been a pretty powerful blow to take — and to absorb — but I think you're right.'

'I still have the second of the two things that I brought back from Milo's house. It's a tape recording. But if you don't mind, I'll bring both the player and tape in and then leave you to it. I think it's something very personal and specifically for you.'

'I'd like to listen to it very much.'

★ ★ ★

It was almost an hour later that Emma dared to reach out and press 'Play' on the tape recorder.

During that hour, Emma had run through in her own mind the full sequence of amazing events that had culminated in her being where she was at this precise moment.

Then, steeling herself for the emotional impact, she took a deep breath and pressed the 'Play' button. Closing her eyes, she prepared once more to hear Milo's voice, speaking only to her, telling of his everlasting love and adoration — of their oneness.

Now, Emma was reliving that stolen week of bliss in the autumn of 'fifty-four, but from Milo's perspective. She was listening to his words, understanding his feelings, his reactions, and knowing his thoughts, down to the finest detail.

As the tape rolled towards the end, he told Emma something else which she did not know until that moment. It had been added to the main body of the tape, rather like a postscript on a letter as Milo had struggled

272

ineffectually to overcome his brain tumour. And Emma's heart bled for him as she experienced his pain and despair as he prepared to leave Wendy.

However, the final sentences were for Emma alone.

'Today my darling Emma, Blakeley, our solicitor from Nottingham, came to see me.

'I have instructed him that my wish is to be cremated and that my ashes be set in a safe place to await, if you so wish, my dearest, the linking with your own when your time comes.

'Although we were not able to be together very long in this lifetime, our earthly bodies may perhaps, at last, mingle and become one forever, for all eternity and beyond.

'But now I want you to go forward, enjoy your children, enjoy the rest of your life. I wish only the very best for you.'

But Emma was still reliving her time in the log cabin, recalling everything about Milo, down to even the tiniest details, and the thoughts played on scent memory. She seemed to smell a subtle drift of fragrance across the quiet bedroom, delightfully fresh, sweet, yet non-feminine.

The gentle, evocative smell recalled in her mind an image of a wood at dawn with the early sunlight glistening golden through the rising mist, highlighting the bluebells, the spring-green leaves on firm, brown branches, brown like Milo's arms — strong, tanned, yet still vulnerable to love. How they had softened to enfold her, to draw her to him.

And in his arms, she'd buried her face into the hollow of his shoulder, wishing she could hold him forever. Milo's distinctive smell had filled her nostrils, drowning her in its embrace. The freshness of winds blowing over wild moors, salt spray from tides, newly planed wood, the warmth of amber, all were contained.

The smell encapsulated the very essence of Milo.

And Emma knew as she closed her eyes and breathed in deeply, surrendering, she could always draw on the beautiful memory, Milo was beside her as close now as he had ever been when alive.

It was true, love did not die as mortal flesh did.

She brought her attention back as Milo's voice on the tape broke into her reverie, taking her by surprise.

'I'm not going to say goodbye, my darling Emma. You are always in my thoughts. We have never been apart — shall never be apart. I love you now, in my last days, and forever.'

As his words ended she could hear playing

softly in the background, Strauss's 'Blue Danube.'

'Milo,' she whispered, 'you have proved to me the power of love. Whenever I need you close, I shall think of you — and you'll be here. God bless, my darling.'

Thalia held the tea tray balanced on the palm of her hand and tapped on Emma's bedroom door.

'Come in.'

She angled the tray round the bedroom door and went into the room. 'I didn't want to disturb you if you were still listening to the tape, Mother.'

'Oh, Thalia, I have listened to it. You were quite right, it was specifically for me.'

'Hmmmm,' Thalia nodded as she poured tea, 'I rather thought so. I didn't want to intrude. It hasn't upset you has it?'

'No, not upset me, darling.' Emma shook her head. 'Touched me, yes, very deeply. What Milo has told me is unique and so precious.'

'May I know?'

'I think you have a right to know, you're his daughter.'

When her mother finished speaking, Thalia said softly, 'Oh, I think that's wonderful. I'm so glad I went to see Steve. If I hadn't you wouldn't have known of Milo's last wishes.'

'Steve?'

Thalia blushed. 'You're not the only woman in this house to have a secret.'

'Really? I'm intrigued.'

'Steve's the man who took me to Milo's house to see about the photograph album. He's Milo's half-brother — and the man I love.'

Emma whitened. She pressed a hand to her lips. 'But it cannot be . . . you could never marry . . . ' She closed her eyes. 'Oh dear God, what have you done?'

'It's all right, Mother, truly, it is.'

'How can it be . . . ?' Emma's voice rose in distress.

'Mother, listen to me,' Thalia said urgently. 'Milo was adopted. His mother and father were not his natural parents. Steve is Milo's half-brother, yes, but — *he is not a blood relative*. Do you understand what I'm saying?'

Slowly, the colour began to return to Emma's cheeks. 'Oh, my darling, I couldn't have borne it, if you had to go through the same experience . . . to be forbidden to spend your life with the man you love. It isn't a sentence I'd pass on any woman.'

Thalia poured out more tea. She passed a cup to Emma. 'Drink this, you've had a shock and you're still weak. I ought not to have told you.'

Emma sipped the hot, reviving tea. 'No.' She shook her head. 'I'm so glad, so relieved, you did. Before you told me about Steve, I was very concerned for you, particularly for your future. But not now. Everything will fall into its rightful place. You think you are the only person in the world who knows your secret, Thalia, but you are wrong.'

Thalia froze. 'How could you know?'

'Because . . . I'm your mother.'

20

Thalia set down her cup of tea on the bedside cabinet with an unsteady hand. 'What do you want to do?'

'Right now,' Emma said firmly, 'I want to speak to the solicitor on the telephone. If you would be so good as to find his number for me.'

Thalia, her thoughts in turmoil, fetched the telephone directory. She flicked through, found the number and dialled.

Downstairs the doorbell rang.

She passed the phone to her mother. 'It's ringing out.' Grateful for an opportunity to steady her thoughts, she ran downstairs to open the front door. When she saw who it was, her heart turned over. Steve was standing there, grinning widely.

'Steve,' she whispered, 'what are you doing here?'

'Taking the bull by the horns, my darling. May I come in?'

'Yes, yes, of course.' Flustered, she stepped back.

'Is there somewhere we can have a word, privately?'

'No-one's in the kitchen. My brothers will be out for two or three hours yet.'

'Good. I wouldn't mind a cup of tea.'

Despite the traumatic events of the last three days, she felt bubbles of joy rise within her at the sight of him. It was the fizz of a bottle of freshly opened champagne — bright, clear, exhilarating.

Without waiting for an answer, he took her hand and drew her down the hall. 'This the kitchen?' He angled his head round the half-opened door. 'Yes, good. Come in here, I've something I want to show you.'

Wonderingly, Thalia followed. 'What is it?'

'This.' He slid a hand into his jacket and took a foolscap envelope from his inside pocket. Go on, open it.'

Thalia drew out the thick sheet of paper inside. There was a covering letter with it but Steve shook his head.

'No, don't bother with that. Read the other document.'

Obediently, Thalia read, 'Decree Absolute' — and stopped. 'Yours?'

'Yes, mine. That,' he flicked the piece of paper with a fingernail, 'says I am now a free man. Well,' he grinned wider than ever, 'if you can call it being free when I'm already head over heels in love with another woman.'

He grabbed for her but Thalia lifted a

hand. 'Wait. I've something to tell you first. It should have been said earlier, but, here goes.' She told him her secret.

And then they were in each other's arms, laughing, almost crying, kissing — totally oblivious to the world.

★ ★ ★

It was fully ten minutes later that Thalia remembered the phone call to the solicitors. With the greatest reluctance, she extricated herself from Steve's embrace. 'There's something I have to do. Come on with me, please, I want you to meet my mother.'

'Mrs Emma Wetherford?'

'That's right.' Thalia laughed at his grave expression. 'She doesn't bite.'

Together, they climbed the stairs. She tapped on the bedroom door and led Steve in.

'Have I a visitor?' Emma asked, looking from her daughter to Steve.

'Mother, I want you to meet someone. This is Steve Viceroy. Steve, this is my mother, Mrs Emma Wetherford.'

Steve bent forward and shook her hand firmly. 'I'm delighted to meet you.'

'And you are Milo's half-brother?'

'That's correct.'

'Haaaa,' Emma murmured, 'life coming full circle.'

She looked at him with keen interest. 'I have to thank you for taking Thalia to Milo's house. She brought me the photograph album and tape.'

He nodded. 'Have you had a chance to have a look at the album, or listen to the tape?'

'We've done both,' said Emma. 'Well, Thalia hasn't actually listened to the tape but there was a relevant piece that I felt she should know. I also feel that, as his half-brother, you should know about it, too.' She indicated the telephone by the side of the bed.

'Thalia, darling, I've spoken to Mr Blakeley, the solicitor. He says if I write an authorisation, they are prepared to release the package that Milo left for me. Apparently, it's in their strong room.'

'Blakely's our family solicitor.' Steve raised an eyebrow. 'Could you fill me in on what this is?'

'It's delicate,' Emma said. 'Are you aware that just before Milo died, he asked this firm of solicitors to come to the house so that he could make his will?'

'Yes,' Steve said hesitantly. 'I knew he had but I really don't know what was drawn up except that Milo made provision to have

Wendy looked after — she's badly handicapped, you see.'

'He asked that he be cremated,' Emma went on gently, 'and that his ashes be held until either I had died or I'd reached the point when I tried to contact him again.'

'And then?'

'I was to be allowed instant access and given the urn containing Milo's ashes. They're prepared to release it this afternoon if I write out an authorisation. If Thalia wouldn't mind going to fetch it.' The appeal in her voice was clear.

Thalia stepped forward, taking her mother's hands. 'Of course I shall go and collect the urn for you, Mother.' She looked enquiringly at Steve.

'And I'll come with you,' he said promptly, 'just to make sure that everything's handed over correctly. Which I'm sure it will be.'

'You will come straight back here?'

'Straight back, I promise, Mother.'

Emma sighed gently and relaxed back against the pillows.

'I'll take us both in my car.' Steve took charge. 'I know exactly where the solicitors' offices are. We should be back in just over an hour.'

★   ★   ★

282

'I had no idea you were holding Milo's ashes,' Steve said, as Mr Blakely scanned Emma's authorisation. 'I naturally thought Wendy had them.'

'Mr Kent's express wishes, Mr Viceroy, were that after probate, we retained the ashes until they were claimed by Mrs Emma Wetherford.'

'I wish I had known . . . ' Steve frowned.

'Mr Kent requested that I did not divulge the information.' Mr Blakely gave a discreet cough. 'Our client's wishes are paramount.'

'Of course.' Steve held out his hand. 'Thank you for all you've done on behalf of our family.'

'We are at your service, Mr Viceroy, at any time.' The solicitor shook his hand warmly. 'I'm very pleased that Mr Kent's ashes are returning to the family.' He handed Thalia a sealed box. 'My good wishes to your mother.'

Thalia reached out with trembling hands and reverently took the box containing her father's ashes. 'Thank you. Thank you so much.'

They drove back to Alney in silence. As Steve turned in at the gates, Thalia said, 'I can't wait to give the urn to Mother. What an emotional experience for her.'

'It looks as though she has visitors.' Steve

nodded to an estate car parked by the front door.

'Oh no,' Thalia smiled, 'that's just my three brothers, they said tea-time but they're back a bit early.'

Inside the hall, she turned to Steve. 'I'd like you to give the ashes to Mother.' Before he could begin to protest, she added, 'It's only right, Milo was your brother.'

'If you're sure, I'd like to — very much.'

'I'm sure.'

Steve kissed her tenderly. 'I'd be honoured. I really appreciate it.'

They went upstairs and Thalia tapped on the bedroom door as she went in. Steve followed behind, holding the box.

Adam, Ian and Simon were assembled around Emma's bed.

When introductions had been made, Ian enquired, 'What relation did you say you were to Milo?'

'Half-brother.'

There was a short, uneasy silence.

'Milo was adopted — we're not blood relations,' Steve said. A collective sigh of relief was audible.

Emma reached out with both hands for the box that Steve held. 'Please . . . '

He gave it to her.

Before unsealing the lid, Emma looked up

at her three sons. 'Inside this box is the urn containing Milo's ashes.' Then, looking at their daughter, added, 'I've already put your brothers in the picture.'

The atmosphere was charged now as they all waited for Emma to undo the box.

Adam stepped forward. 'Here, Mother, let me help you with the seal.'

'Thanks, darling.' Emma carefully raised the lid. Inside was a bronze urn. Reverently, she lifted the urn out and held it — staring at it without speaking for a long time.

The others looked on in respectful silence.

Emma held it out to Steve. 'Perhaps you could put it down for me. Over there, please, on the windowsill, in the sunshine.' Steve crossed the room and did as she asked.

'There's something else in the box, Mother,' Thalia prompted.

Emma dragged her gaze away from the urn where it now stood, catching the late westering sun causing the bronze to give off a warm glow. 'So there is,' she murmured and picked up a small package. Quickly unwrapping it, a beatific smile spread over her face, illuminating it from the inside so that she, too, seemed to give off an inner glow.

Wordlessly, she passed it to Thalia. Mindful of the four men craning their necks to see what it was, Thalia read the handwritten label. 'The Blue Danube by Strauss.' Thalia's eyes filled with tears as she handed the recording back to her mother.

'I don't know if this is the right time to tell you at all,' she began, 'but it feels like the right time. Steve has just asked me to marry him — and I have accepted.'

'Oh darling!' Emma reached for her daughter, hugging her close. 'I'm so, so pleased.'

'Yes, indeed.' Adam shook Steve's hand warmly and murmured their congratulations.

'You need looking after, Sis, I've been saying it for years, but you never took any notice,' said Ian.

Simon laughed. 'Welcome to the family, Steve. Of course, we shall expect red hot tips for the races, mind.'

Emma smiled round happily at her offspring. Giving Thalia a big hug she said, 'Darling, aren't you going to tell us your other piece of news?'

Thalia stood up, taking a deep breath and looking at her brothers. 'I expect you'll be shocked, but not too shocked, I hope. I'm going to have a baby — Steve's baby.' She giggled, a little embarrassed now. 'You'll all be uncles.'

'Phew! You don't waste time, do you?' said Ian, raising his eyebrows and looking directly at Steve.

'Well, I thought I'd better ask her to marry me,' he said flippantly, 'before I had all three of you on to me — not to mention Emma pointing a shotgun at my head.' They all began laughing.

Finally, Thalia said to her mother, 'I hadn't told anyone, not even Steve, until earlier this afternoon in the kitchen. But you knew, didn't you, Mother? Tell me, how on earth *did* you know?'

Emma smiled, 'I didn't know, not for sure. But when a woman is expecting a baby, her face changes subtly, especially around her eyes. And there's a sort of aura of tender protectiveness around her. Plus I had noticed, Thalia, you were secretly trying to cope with morning sickness . . . '

'You never let on you suspected, though.'

'You're a grown woman, my darling. Your life is your own. And I knew you would tell me when you were ready. But, yes, it made me very concerned for your future.'

'Mrs Wetherford, 'Steve said earnestly, 'you don't need to worry. I will look after Thalia — and our baby.'

'I'm sure you will.' Emma laid her hand over his. 'This baby is so special. What better reason could I have for coming out of the coma than to see my daughter's new baby?'

She held her arms out with joy, encompassing all of them. 'And Thalia's not just my daughter, she's Milo's daughter, too. The baby is Milo's grandchild.'

Epilogue

1999

A stiff, offshore wind was blowing. It rippled the grass growing on the cliff top above the bay at Sandsend. Higher still, the sky was a particularly vivid blue for early December.

Three people, two men and a woman, were climbing the cliff path. The older man held the woman's hand whilst the young man went ahead. Reaching the top, they paused briefly for breath before stepping out briskly along the very edge of the cliff top. For a short distance they walked purposefully before their footsteps slowly faltered and they came to a standstill, turning to look at the beach below and out across the sea where the waves rose and fell, creamed and ran up the sands in long, white fingers. The beach was deserted.

'What do you think, Thalia?' The older man turned to her. 'Is this a suitable spot?'

She squeezed his hand and looked lovingly up into his face. 'Very suitable.'

'Was this the beach, Dad?' asked the young man. 'The beach where my grandparents rode the horses?'

Steve nodded, 'Yes, Milo, this was the very beach.'

Both men looked across at the woman and Milo held out the bronze urn that he had carried up to the top of the cliff. 'Yours, I think, Mum.'

Thalia took the urn from her son. She turned and looked out over the sea. 'Wherever you are, Mother and . . . Milo — I shall always think of you as Milo, as well as being my father — wherever you are, I know you're together. As above — so below.'

She took the lid from the urn containing the combined ashes and seemed to hear again the music that had been played in church at the end of Emma's funeral, a few days ago. Casting a glance at her husband and son, she saw they were both softly whistling the haunting strains of Strauss's 'Blue Danube'. As she listened, she felt the sadness within her fade away.

'God bless you both,' she whispered and tipped the contents of the urn over the cliff top.

The strong wind caught the white dust and bore it away across the beach and far out to sea.

We do hope that you have enjoyed reading this large print book.

Did you know that all of our titles are available for purchase?

We publish a wide range of high quality large print books including:
Romances, Mysteries, Classics
General Fiction
Non Fiction and Westerns

Special interest titles available in large print are:
The Little Oxford Dictionary
Music Book
Song Book
Hymn Book
Service Book

Also available from us courtesy of Oxford University Press:
Young Readers' Dictionary
(large print edition)
Young Readers' Thesaurus
(large print edition)

For further information or a free brochure, please contact us at:
Ulverscroft Large Print Books Ltd.,
The Green, Bradgate Road, Anstey,
Leicester, LE7 7FU, England.
Tel: (00 44) 0116 236 4325
Fax: (00 44) 0116 234 0205

PHOTO FINISH

Glenis Wilson

Black pearl smuggling and an abducted ex-government scientist seem totally unconnected and a million miles away from English horse-racing — but as Jim Crack, ex-jump jockey, now private eye, discovers, they are not. As the attention swings between the race-courses of England and Malta, Jim finds himself caught up in a web of danger, intrigue and romance, and he is forced to confront the dark shadows from his own past. The suspense builds up, as twist follows twist, into a totally unexpected, explosive climax.

BLOOD ON THE TURF

Glenis Wilson

When Jack Hunter is badly injured in a race accident, his daughter, Tal, finds herself having to take over his rides and the running of their racing stables. To keep the stables afloat, winners are required on the track; Tal is determined to get them, but someone is equally determined she will not. Ancient family skeletons are rattled from their cupboards and Tal's world is shaken apart when she discovers just who the 'someone' is.

THE WATER IS WIDE

Liz Gilbey

Artist Mikki Webster takes her beloved narrow-boat, *Serendipity*, on a holiday tour of Britain's waterways, stopping in at Bleakhall to visit her brother Jonny and his wife Tracy. The couple have their hands full — renovating their canal-side cottage, launching their new careers, and coping with an imminent baby as well as their rebellious teenager Katie. When Katie has a serious motorbike accident, Mikki stays moored beside Wharf Cottage in order to lend a hand. But sparks fly when Mikki, working at the boatyard, encounters Bill Rankin — the pop star she had fallen in love with all those years ago . . .

BEYOND REASON

Gwen Kirkwood

Young Janet Scott loves books and learning, and is happy living at the schoolhouse where her grandfather is the dominie. Her world is shattered when he dies and the new schoolmaster's petty cruelty becomes intolerable. Sent to work for farmer Wull Foster, Janet becomes the target of his dangerous lechery, and escapes. Taken in by the kind philanthropist Josiah Saunders, an old friend of her grandfather's, she is pitched into a dilemma when he offers her the security of an amiable but passionless marriage. For her heart belongs to another: her childhood friend, the penniless lawyer's clerk Fingal McLauchlan . . .

APHRODITE'S ISLAND

Hilary Green

1955: The island of Cyprus is torn apart by EOKA's insurrection against British rule. Seventeen-year-old Ariadne's family are deeply involved in the rebellion, guarding hidden caches of rifles to arm the militants. But when British soldier Stephen Allenby arrives to search their house, a spark ignites between him and Ariadne: despite their divided loyalties, the two fall in love . . . 1973: Back in England, Stephen labours under the twin shadows of a strained marriage and miserable job. Then the rise of EOKA-B sends him back to Cyprus as a foreign correspondent and information-gatherer, all the while searching the island for the memories of his youth . . .